10

SUGAR CREEK GANG
The MYSTERY THIEF

Paul Hutchens

MOODY PRESS
CHICAGO

PREFACE

Hi—from a member of the Sugar Creek Gang!

It's just that I don't know which one I am. When I was good, I was Little Jim. When I did bad things—well, sometimes I was Bill Collins or even mischievous Poetry.

You see, I am the daughter of Paul Hutchens, and I spent many an hour listening to him read his manuscript as far as he had written it that particular day. I went along to the north woods of Minnesota, to Colorado, and to the various other places he would go to find something different for the Gang to do.

Now the years have passed—more than fifty, actually. My father is in heaven, but the Gang goes on. All thirty-six books are still in print and now are being updated for today's readers with input from my five children, who also span the decades from the '50s to the '70s.

The real Sugar Creek is in Indiana, and my father and his six brothers were the original Gang. But the idea of the books and their ministry were and are the Lord's. It is He who keeps the Gang going.

PAULINE HUTCHENS WILSON

1

I was so angry because of the things I'd read in the crazy letter I had in my hand that, when Mom called me to hurry up and come into the house because one of the gang wanted to talk to me on the phone, I couldn't even be glad, the way I usually am. Nearly always when Mom yells for me to come to the phone, I am so pleased I just drop whatever I am doing and run like a Sugar Creek cottontail straight to the house, my heart pounding and my mind imagining all kinds of important things I'll probably hear.

But honestly, that letter was terrible. I took another glance at it and shoved in into my pocket—not that I'd have any trouble remembering it. I wouldn't. I'd probably never forget it as long as I lived—that is, if I lived very long, for that letter, written in the craziest handwriting I ever saw, said that I was a roughneck and that I was to beware! That means to look out for something or somebody. It also sounded as if whoever wrote it was terribly mad at me for something I had done or was supposed to have done.

It was a crazy time of the day to get a letter too—just before dark. And it hadn't been brought by our mail carrier either. He came every morning either in his car or sometimes, in the winter, in a sleigh with bells jingling on his horse's harness. But the letter I held in my pocket had been shoved into our mailbox just a little while ago by some strange-looking man who had sneaked up out of the woods and put it into the box out beside the road, and then had hurried away into the woods again.

"Who is it?" I called to Mom when I reached our kitchen door, ready to dash through to the living room, where I'd make a dive across our nice new rug straight for the phone by the window.

"Wait a minute, Bill Collins!" Mom stopped me with her voice as if I'd been shot. I reached for the broom without even being told to and started sweeping the snow off my boots—I had walked in the deep snow in our yard because I had been reading the crazy letter and hadn't paid any attention to where I was walking.

"Is it Poetry?" I asked her, taking a last two or three quick swipes with the brown-strawed broom. I hoped it was Poetry, the barrel-shaped member of the Sugar Creek Gang, who knew 101 poems by heart and was always quoting one of them at the wrong time. Whenever I was mad or glad or had a secret, Poetry was the first one of our gang of seven boys I wanted to talk to.

Just as I was about to say "Hello" into the telephone, Mom said, "Not more than one minute, Bill. I'm expecting a long-distance call from Wally's father."

I'd forgotten all about my cousin Wally, who lived in the city and had a new baby sister. Mom was going there that night to stay for a few days or a week, and Dad and I were going to "batch it," which means we'd have to do our own cooking and even wash our own dishes while she was away.

We hardly ever had a long-distance phone call at our house, so whenever we did, it seemed very important. Just the same, I didn't like to hear her say for me not to talk too long. Mom and Dad were always saying that whenever one of the gang called me up or I called one of them, which means that we maybe did sometimes talk too long.

Anyway, I grabbed up the phone and said, "Hello!"

Sure enough, it was Poetry, my very best pal, and his ducklike voice on the other end of the line made me feel good all over.

"Hi, there, Bill!" the ducklike voice said. "This is Poetry. I've just made up a poem about our new teacher. Want to hear it?"

I did, and I didn't. As you maybe know, we got a new teacher in our one-room school right after Christmas vacation. His name was Mr. Black, and he was maybe forty years old and had some of his hair gone from the middle of the top of his head. We had all been pretty disappointed when we lost our pretty woman teacher, and none of us felt very glad about a change.

In fact, some of us hadn't behaved ourselves very well that first day, and I especially had had trouble. On top of that, Dad and I'd had an interesting experience in our wood-shed when I got home from school. So I had already made up my mind to be respectful to Mr. Black, the way any decent boy ought to be to his teacher.

I wanted to hear Poetry's poem, of course, but mostly I wanted to tell him about the letter I had in my pocket, which called the Sugar Creek Gang a bunch of roughnecks, which none of us boys was trying to be.

"What's the matter?" Poetry squawked. "Don't you want to hear my poem? What are you so quiet for?"

"I was just thinking," I said.

"About what?"

"Oh, just something," I told him.

"Not too long," Mom said behind me.

"I won't," I said to her.

"Won't what?" Poetry said.

"Won't talk very long. We're getting a long-distance call in a minute, so we can't talk too long."

"Want to hear my new poem?"

"Sure," I said, "but hurry up, because I have something very important to tell you."

I could just imagine how Poetry would gasp when he heard the crazy letter I had in my pocket.

If I hadn't had that experience with Dad in our woodshed, I think I would have laughed at Poetry's poem about our new teacher, which went like this:

"The Sugar Creek Gang had the
    strangest of teachers
And 'Black' his name was called;
His round red face had the homeliest
    features—
He was fat and forty and bald.

"The very first day . . ."

"Can't you hurry?" Mom said behind me. "We're expecting the call right this minute!"

"I've got to hurry," I interrupted Poetry. "We're expecting a long-distance call. My cousin Wally has got a new baby sister and—"

"Oh, all right then," Poetry said, "if you don't think my poem is important—"

"But it is," I said. "It's—why, it's even funny. But I have something even more important to quick tell you. It's about a letter which somebody just shoved into our—into our—" I suddenly sneezed because of the smell of the sulfur that was in the room after Mom had lit a match. I always sneezed when somebody lit a match near me.

"I hope you don't have a cold," Poetry said, "because you're supposed to come over to my house and sleep tonight. That's why I called you up. Mother says for you to stay at our house while your mother is away at your cousin Wally's house."

Well, that sounded good. So in spite of the fact that I wanted to tell Poetry about the letter in my pocket and also Poetry wanted to finish his poem about our new teacher, Mr. Black, and also mainly because Mom wanted me to stop talking, I turned and asked her, "Can I stay at Poetry's house tonight?"

"Certainly," she said. "I've already planned that for you. Now, will you hang up?"

"I've got to hang up," I said to Poetry, "but I'll be over just as soon as I can. Mom says I can."

"Bring the letter with you," he said, "and bring your father's big long flashlight. There's something very important we have to do tonight."

Boy, oh, boy, when Poetry said to bring Dad's flashlight and that there was something very important we had to do, my imagination started to fly in every direction. Poetry and I had had some of the most exciting experiences at night when I had my dad's long flashlight with me. Once we'd caught a bank robber who was digging for treasure down by the old sycamore tree not far from Poetry's house.

"Sure I'll bring the flashlight," I said, "and the letter too. It's the craziest letter I ever read. It says I'm a roughneck and that all the Sugar Creek Gang are roughnecks and—"

"Hey—" Poetry cut in, saying real saucily to somebody, "Hang up! This line is busy!"

Maybe I'd better explain to you that we had what is called a "party line," and about a half dozen families all used it but had different rings. Anybody who wanted to could listen to anybody he wanted to, just by lifting up his own telephone receiver. But that is called *eavesdropping* and is considered very impolite and a breach of etiquette and everything.

I knew what Poetry meant, for I'd heard the sound myself. Somebody somewhere had lifted a telephone receiver and was listening to us.

And then Mom came across the room to where I was and said very politely into our telephone, "Hello, Poetry. We'll bring Bill over in the car after a while. He'll have to hang up now because we're waiting for a long-distance call."

I pushed the phone receiver up to Mom's ear, so we could both hear Poetry talk back.

"Surely, Mrs. Collins," he said politely. "I'm sorry I talked so long."

"You boys be good and don't get into any more mischief," Mom said pleasantly.

"We won't, Mrs. Collins," Poetry promised. "And I hope you have a very nice trip. Tell Wally I said hello."

"I will," Mom said. "Will you call your mother to the phone? I've something important to tell her."

"Surely," Poetry said. "So long, Bill. I'll be seeing you pretty soon."

"He's a nice boy," Mom said to me, and I knew by the way she said it that she wasn't angry at me for using what is called a little friendly sarcasm a while ago. That is the easiest way not to have any trouble in a family—if nobody takes anybody too seriously, Dad says.

Boy, oh, boy! I thought. I darted out of our

living room toward the kitchen and was going upstairs to pack my pajamas into my small brown suitcase, when Mom called, "Your pajamas are all ready, Bill, there by the radio."

Then she started talking to Poetry's mom, saying different things, which I didn't pay much attention to, such as "We're very sorry, Lita." Lita was Poetry's mom's first name. "You know how much we'd like to be there. I'm sure you'll have a wonderful time. But maybe we can come over for an evening after I get back . . . New babies just don't wait for neighborhood get-togethers! We know you'll all have a wonderful time . . . Yes, that's right . . . Well, look after my boy, and help him keep out of mischief."

It wasn't exactly necessary for my mom to say that, but I didn't get mad at her for saying it because I was already as mad as I could get at whoever had written the crazy note about the gang and me.

I had started to pick up my suitcase by the radio, and Mom was just finishing what she was saying to Poetry's mom when I heard her say, "I've pinned your brooch to Bill's pajamas. It certainly is beautiful. I wish I had one like it. Maybe when I'm in the city, I can look around in the stores a bit . . . Oh, that's all right, Lita . . . No, I wouldn't think of it. I might lose it, and then how would I feel? No, I'll just send it along with Bill. We'll bring him over right away . . . Sorry . . . No . . . Well, good-bye . . . What? . . . Oh, yes . . ."

I wasn't paying much attention, except to hear that she was sending something along with me in my suitcase for Mrs. Thompson. I was in a hurry to get to Poetry's house, so I said, "We're waiting for a long-distance call, Mom. Can't you hang up now and—"

Almost right away she hung up, and also almost right away after that the phone rang again, and it was Wally's dad.

After *that*, we all dived into whatever had to be done before Mom and Dad could get going. They actually left the dishes unwashed for a change. Dad adjusted the oil burner in the big stove in our front room, and in almost no time we were all in the car on our way down the already dark road toward Poetry's house.

"I'll be driving back late tonight or else early tomorrow," Dad said, "so you won't need to bother about doing chores. You just go straight to school from Poetry's house in the morning."

"Poetry's mother will fix your lunch for you," Mom said to me.

I was in the backseat of our two-door sedan, with Mom's luggage and my small suitcase beside me. Mom and Charlotte Ann, my little one-year-old baby sister, were in front so they could keep warm near the heater.

It was a beautiful night. Big lazy flakes of snow were falling, and the headlights of the car certainly were pretty as they shone down the road. The snowflakes seemed to come from somewhere out in the dark, dropping down into the light of the headlights and then disappearing again, sort of like fireflies in the summer along Sugar Creek.

I had Dad's flashlight and was switching it on and off, shooting it out through the back window at the trees in the woods and toward Sugar Creek.

Pretty soon we came to the little lane that leads to Poetry's house.

"You don't need to turn in," I said. "I can walk the rest of the way."

"Maybe we *had* better go right on," Dad said. "You have the flashlight . . ."

"Sure," I said. "I'll just follow the lane." I had on my boots, and it'd only take me a few minutes to get there, I thought. And my suitcase wasn't heavy.

I could see the light in Poetry's front window. They'd fixed up their basement into a nice recreation room, so he and I would play Ping-Pong and maybe checkers and do a lot of interesting things before it would be time to go to bed. And I'd be sure to show him the crazy letter I had in my pocket.

Thinking of that reminded me that I hadn't shown the letter to my parents yet, and I knew I should before they went away. In fact, I had been thinking all along the way that I had better show it to them before they went to Wally's house, so I spoke up. "Want to read the letter I just found in our mailbox?"

"A letter?" Mom said.

We were still stopped at the gate to Poetry's lane.

"If it won't take too long," she said. "We're a long distance from Wally's house right now, and they wanted us to hurry."

"Here it is," I said and started to hand it over the front seat to Mom, snapping on the ceiling light at the same time.

"It's too dark to read without my glasses," she said. "You read it to us with the flashlight."

This is what I read to them:

Dear William Collins:

Your son better treat my boy decent or I'll shake the living daylights out of him. It's a pity a family cant move into a naborhood without a gang of ruffnecks beating up on his boy. I don't know if you are the ones who took my wife to church last night or not, but somebody did while I was away from home and you cant believe a thing she says about me. You mind your own business and I'll mind mine. My wife has enuff high and mity ideas without going to some fancy church to get more. If she would obey her husband like the Bible says, it would do her some good to read the Bible, but she don't. Your boy is the worst ruffneck in the whole Sugar Creek Gang of ruffnecks, so beware.

When I finished reading, both my parents were very quiet, while Charlotte Ann babbled and wiggled and tried to stand up in Mom's lap and look at me. She was also trying to get her hands on the flashlight and the letter, which I wouldn't let her do.

Then, because Dad was a very good Christian and since talking about prayer or the Bible and things like that was as natural for him as for a boy to talk about slingshots and marbles, he said. "We'll pray for whoever wrote it, and maybe the Lord will change his heart."

But Mom was bothered about that part of the letter that called the Sugar Creek Gang a bunch of roughnecks—and especially the part that called me the worst roughneck in the whole gang. She said, "Are you sure you and Shorty Long haven't been having trouble? Are you sure you have been treating him like a new boy in the neighborhood *ought* to be treated?"

As you maybe know, Shorty hadn't lived long in our neighborhood, and he and I hadn't been getting along at all. We'd had a fight the very first time we met and had had another one that very day. But he had started both of them.

"Of course that letter is from his father," Dad said.

"Answer me," Mom said.

But at that moment Charlotte Ann managed to squirm far enough out of Mom's arms to reach over the front seat and get hold of the letter I had in my hand. She held onto it like a bulldog holding onto another dog's throat—or like a snapping turtle holding onto a barefoot boy's big toe.

"Let loose!" I said to Charlotte Ann. "This letter is very important." I pried her soft little hand loose, which she didn't like very well. She started to cry, so I didn't have a chance to answer Mom.

"Answer me," Mom said again, getting in her words while Charlotte Ann was taking in a breath right before her next howl. *Such an unearthly noise to make in the night*, I thought. *You'd think we were a bunch of kidnappers or something.*

I answered Mom, though. "Shorty Long and I have had trouble, but I'm trying to act like I ought to." When I said that, it seemed to me I'd been giving Shorty Long just what a new boy deserved, especially one who needed a good licking by somebody who was big enough to do it. I had proved I was that very day.

Then Dad, who is always giving me good commonsense advice—which is sometimes hard for me to take but good for me—said, "Remember, every boy has a soul, Bill, and that he needs a Savior, and sometimes a boy needs a friend, too, before he will become a Christian."

"Yes sir," I said, and I knew he was right, although I wasn't in a mood right that minute to admit it.

"Well," Mom said, "we'd better be going on." Her voice suddenly was very kind and not a bit worried as she said, "I'll drop you men a card every day I'm gone. Be sure to keep the dishes washed at least once a day, and remember to sweep off the snow before coming into the house on my nice new living room rug."

I knew Mom was talking to me mostly, because Dad hardly ever needed to be reminded about using the broom on his boots, Mom having already trained him to do it.

I reached over and shook hands with Dad, gave Mom a short kiss, and was about to give Charlotte Ann one when she grabbed hold of my cap and pulled it off, which made me wonder whatever makes baby sisters so ill-mannered anyway.

I got my cap again and was ready to go when Mom said, "There's something in your suitcase for Mrs. Thompson. She knows about it, so be sure to remember to give it to her."

"I will," I said, hardly hearing her, because that didn't seem half as important as the letter I was going to show to Poetry when I got there.

We all said good-bye, I slipped out of the car, and a jiffy later they were gone. Their lights were like a big snowplow pushing back the dark for their car to follow it through. And there I was alone at the side of the road, with the big lazy snowflakes falling all around me and upon me and all of a sudden feeling lonesome.

Then I turned, shining the flashlight around in a circle at the trees in the woods on one side of Poetry's lane and at the bent and twisted cornstalks of the cornfield on the other side. I started down the lane toward Poetry's house, wondering why he hadn't put on his boots and warm clothes and come out to meet me at the gate.

I had the letter and my little suitcase in one hand and the flashlight in the other. I could hardly wait till I got to Poetry's house.

All of a sudden I heard a weird sound out in the woods not far from me. It sounded like a screech owl, and it went *shay-shay-shay-a-a-a*. It scared me stiff and made me want to run. But it was almost an eighth of a mile up the lane yet before I would get to Poetry's house. There really wasn't any sense in my being scared. I'd heard screech owls many a time at night, and they weren't dangerous. Dad says they are the farmers' friends. They eat mice and cutworms and things.

But for some reason, I *was* scared. The woods beside which I was walking was the same woods out of which that strange-looking man in old work clothes had come walking to put that letter in our mailbox. And even though I had the flashlight and could see where I was going, I kept remembering the first and last sentences in the letter, which were: "Your son better treat my boy decent, or I'll shake the living daylights out of him. . . . Your boy is the worst ruffneck in the whole Sugar Creek Gang of ruffnecks, so beware."

The owl let out another moaning, quavering wail. *Shay-shay-shay-a-a-a*. And I actually felt my hair trying to stand on end under my winter cap. That old screech owl must have been in the tree right above me, for it sounded terribly close.

Then, just like that, things began to happen. A gray shadow shot out from behind an evergreen and made a dash for me. Before I could even scream, which I couldn't have done anyway since I was so scared, somebody's strong hand twisted me around and around and gave me a big shove headfirst into a snowdrift.

2

It certainly was no fun lying upside down in a snowdrift and being scared half to death at the same time. I still had Dad's flashlight in my hand, which he always had urged me to be very careful not to lose, but the letter I'd had in my other hand was gone.

While I was trying to untangle myself from myself and scramble out of the snowdrift, somebody yelled down at me fiercely, "You little red-headed runt! Let that be a lesson to you to be careful what you tell people over the phone!"

How'd he know I was redheaded? I wondered. Then I felt how cold my head was and knew my cap was off. I also remembered the sound of somebody picking up a telephone receiver and listening to what Poetry and I were saying.

A lot of voices began yelling from the direction of Poetry's house just then, and it sounded like the whole Sugar Creek Gang. I tell you that was a welcome sound. I didn't have time to wonder why all the gang was there, but I was glad they were coming. I could see a lantern swaying, and at the same time there were different-pitched voices hollering all kinds of things, and I knew it must be the whole gang— or most of it.

The guy who had shoved me into the ditch

must have been scared himself, for quick as a flash he dodged behind the evergreen tree and then ran lickety-split through the snow. I heard the sound of his feet crunching through the underbrush of the woods, and then I couldn't hear him any longer because the gang was making so much noise as they hurried up Poetry's lane to meet me.

I surely was glad to see the gang and also glad that the big bully, whoever he was, was gone. For the first time I noticed I had a pain in my jaw, which meant I must have been hit by his fist or else had got hurt on a tree root or something when I fell into the snowdrift.

I must have lost control for a minute, for when the gang came crunching and yelling up to me in the falling snow, I was actually crying. I was trying not to and hating myself for doing it, because a boy hates to be caught crying by anybody, since people might think he is a sissy or a coward, which I *wasn't*. I was mad at myself for doing it, but for half a minute I couldn't help myself.

So I blurted out to the gang. "Let's get him . . . after him, gang! The dirty crook! He stole my letter and knocked the living daylights out of me, and now he's running away. Come on. Let's get him!"

"Get who?" . . . "What?" . . . "Where is he?" . . . "Who are you talking about?" . . . "'S'matter Bill?" . . . "What you crying about?" . . . "Where's your cap?" . . . "What are you all covered with snow for?"

The gang was firing questions at me like snowballs, and I couldn't answer a one of them because I was still mad. But now that the gang was there, I felt very brave at the same time. I wanted to run after the bully and catch him and have all of us to beat up on him, whoever he was.

Right that minute, I couldn't any more answer all the gang's questions than fly, but, as I said, I felt very brave all of a sudden, and if I had had the bully there, whoever he was, I could have knocked the living daylights out of *him* all by myself. They certainly were a great gang, the best gang a boy ever belonged to, I thought, anywhere in the whole world.

"Here's your cap." Little Jim's voice sounded like a mouse's voice that was very polite. I could see his small, kind face in the light of Poetry's kerosene lantern, and it had that innocent lamblike look that it nearly always has, even when he is being mischievous.

"Thanks, Little Jim," I said, liking him even better than I sometimes do, because he is always doing things like that for me. He is always doing things for his parents, too, without being told, which my mom thinks is the main reason Little Jim is a great guy. Maybe it is.

I shook the snow off and out of my cap and put it on again, not putting the ear flaps down though, because I was pretty hot. Boys nearly always do that to their caps whenever they've gotten warmed up on a cold day or night.

The gang was chattering and chattering and asking excited questions, and I was trying to answer. Big Jim is our leader and the only one of us that has anything on his upper lip that looks like a mustache. And even it doesn't look like one but looks more like the down you see on a little baby pigeon when you look at it in its nest.

All of a sudden Big Jim said, "Quiet, everybody. Let him talk!"

I told them the whole story, all about my cousin Wally, who lived in the city, having a new baby sister. And that Mom had to be taken there by my dad. And that while we were getting ready to go, I'd seen somebody sneak up through the woods from across the road and put something in our mailbox. And how, when I'd gotten it and read it, I saw it was addressed to William Collins, Sr. And . . .

Dragonfly, the pop-eyed member of our gang was standing and shivering beside Poetry, the barrel-shaped member. He was sort of leaning up against him on the side of Poetry that was the other side from which way the wind was blowing. He said, "But—but you aren't William Collins, Senior. That letter was written to your dad."

"Sure," Circus, our monkey-faced acrobat, said, "Dads are seniors, and their kids are juniors."

"Not always," Poetry squawked. "Not when nearly all the children in the home are girls." He was being a little bit sarcastic, because Circus had six sisters and not even one brother to make life easier for him.

Circus looked around as though he was looking for a tree to climb. That was what he'd nearly always rather do than anything else when he had a chance. But there wasn't any tree small enough, so he started catching snowflakes, reaching out and grabbing them and pretending to make a little pile of them in one of his kind of dirty hands.

"Anyway," I began again, "the letter was crazy, and lots of the words were misspelled. It said the Sugar Creek Gang was a bunch of roughnecks, and that I was the worst rough-neck of the whole gang and—"

"You aren't!" Dragonfly piped up. "Poetry is." He shouldn't have said that, because it wasn't any time to be funny. But Dragonfly didn't always know when it was or wasn't time to be funny, since he couldn't help being funny nearly all the time anyway.

I ignored his remark, as did most of the others, and went on with my exciting story, waving my turned-on flashlight around in a circle and saying, "Anyway it sounded like he thought my dad's name was William instead of Theodore, which it is, but the letter said we had to treat his son decently and not beat up on him and—"

"It was Shorty Long's dad who wrote the letter then," Little Jim said.

That sounded right, because the gang, and especially Bill Collins, had had a fight with him that very day, and I'd had one with him about two weeks before, not long after Shorty Long's family had moved into our neighborhood.

I told the rest of what had happened as fast as I could, with different ones of the gang interrupting me every other minute to ask questions. But pretty soon I had the whole thing told—how I'd talked to Poetry on the phone and that somebody had been listening in when I told him about the crazy misspelled letter.

"I heard *two* telephones go up and down," Poetry said, "not just one. There must have been two neighbors listening."

"I heard *three*," Circus said as he stopped catching snowflakes.

"What!" I said. "Were you listening too?"

"Sure, I wanted to call you up and tell you something important, and so I lifted the receiver to see if the line was busy. You and Poetry were already talking. So while you were talking and I was listening, I heard three different telephone receivers go up. And whoever the people were, they were listening to you."

"Maybe one of them was mine," Dragonfly said. "I was going to call you up about something important and—"

"Quiet!" Big Jim ordered. "Let's have the whole story. Go ahead, Bill."

I went ahead and said, "Then when I'd said good-bye to my folks right there by the gate and they had started on down the road on the way to Wally's house, a screech owl let out a terrible wail and scared me half to death. And then, while I was getting over being scared, somebody shot out from behind that fir tree and grabbed the letter out of my hand and shoved me into the ditch. He said, "You little redheaded runt! Let that be a lesson to you to be careful about what you tell people over the telephone!"

"Then it was Shorty Long's dad who was listening in and who wanted the letter back again!" Circus said.

Little Jim said, "I don't think the Longs have any phone, because Mom tried to call there last Saturday to ask Mrs. Long to go to church with us. The telephone was discon—discon—"

"Disconnected," Dragonfly said, and Little Jim said, "Yeah, disconnected."

"Maybe they had it connected again," Circus said, pretending to eat all the snowflakes he had caught. "Maybe they paid their bill."

Circus probably was the only one of the Sugar Creek Gang to know what that might mean, because his dad used to get drunk before he became a Christian. Then they sometimes couldn't pay their telephone bill for a long time and had to have their phone disconnected.

Big Jim spoke then, and in the light of Poetry's lantern, which was smoking a little, I could see that he was thinking about something very seriously. He said, "It couldn't have been Mr. Long listening in on your line. He's not on *your* line. He's on *ours*."

Well, that was that.

Anyway, I was rattling on again, telling them that, whoever it was, he had heard the gang coming and had made a dash for the fir tree, and that I'd heard him running through the woods only a few minutes ago. Telling the gang that and still being mad and also very brave (because the gang was with me), I began to feel my blood getting hot, and I said, "Let's follow his tracks and see where he went. Let's find out who it is!"

And Poetry, who is interested in being a detective someday and is always talking about clues and things, said, "If we had the letter, it would be a good clue."

"We'll have to hurry," Big Jim said, "or this snow will cover up all his tracks," which it would in even just a little while.

"Let's run up to the house and tell my folks we're going to take a walk," Poetry said. "We can leave Bill's suitcase there and—"

Suitcase! I'd forgotten all about it. Something in my mind started whirling. *Where is my suitcase? Why—why—*

"Hey!" I yelled. "Where is my suitcase? Hey! Why, it's gone. It's—that guy must have taken it with him. And it's got my brand-new pair of pajamas in it!"

3

When I shone my dad's flashlight in every direction and couldn't see my little brown suitcase anywhere, I got terribly scared. It not only had my pajamas in it, but all of a sudden I remembered what I'd half heard my mom say on the phone to Poetry's mom. She had pinned Poetry's mom's brooch to my new pajamas. Also I remembered that just as I had stepped out of our car a little while ago, Mom had reminded me that there was something for Mrs. Thompson inside the suitcase.

Boy, oh, boy, I felt even more tangled up in my mind now than I had been, for I realized that the roughneck who had stolen the letter and had knocked the living daylights out of me and had shoved me into the snowdrift had also stolen the suitcase and everything that was in it.

"Come on, gang!" I cried. "Let's trail him in the snow! Let's find out where he went and who he is. And let's lick the living daylights out of him." Then I told the gang what was in the suitcase besides my new pajamas.

Poetry spoke up excitedly. "What? My mom's pretty new brooch was in it? Why—why—why—I bought that for Mom for Christmas! Why—"

Our excitement caught fire like a straw stack out in a field, and we were all ready to make a quick dash straight for the evergreen tree and get started on the guy's trail.

But Big Jim stopped us, pulled back his sleeve, looked at his watch in the light of Poetry's lantern, and said, "We're scheduled to be at Old Man Paddler's cabin at seven o'clock. He's expecting us. Otherwise he can't come tonight!"

Can't come where? Where's he going? I thought and then asked it out loud. I found, by tying together what different ones of the gang said in broken pieces of sentences, that all the Sugar Creek Gang's parents and some other neighbors, as well as Old Man Paddler, were supposed to meet at Poetry's house that night to help celebrate the new furnace and recreation room that Poetry's parents had in their basement. My parents hadn't told me about it, I guess, because I had had some trouble with Dad in the woodshed right after school. Either they had forgotten it later or else maybe Mom and Dad had wanted me to be surprised.

Anyway, a lot of people were coming to Poetry's house after a while, and the gang got to come early so that we would have fun for a while without the parents being present, which boys nearly always like to do.

Besides, some *girls* might come with the different parents, and that would spoil the party for the whole Sugar Creek Gang—except maybe for Big Jim, who wouldn't care if our minister's daughter, Sylvia, came. And maybe even I wouldn't get mad if one of Circus's ordinary-looking sisters named Lucille came along.

She was one of the main reasons I had given Shorty Long a licking that very morning on the way to school, which you already know about if you've read *One Stormy Day*.

According to Big Jim's watch, it wasn't much after six o'clock, and we would have plenty of time to go to the cave near the sycamore tree and follow it far back into the hills to where it came out in the basement of Old Man Paddler's cabin.

"We've got to get Bill's suitcase back and my mom's new brooch!" Poetry said, as excited as I was, and I could see on his face that he also was angry at whoever had stolen the letter and the suitcase and the brooch.

"Here we go, then!" Big Jim said. "Here, Circus. You take Poetry's lantern. And Bill, let me have your flashlight. Circus and I'll lead the way. Come on! We'll have to get going fast before the snow covers up his tracks."

Behind the evergreen tree we all stopped a minute and gathered in a huddle to study the tracks and see if they were from anybody's shoes or boots that we might know.

"See!" Circus said. "His shoes—one of his shoes has a hole in its sole." And sure enough, it had.

"Why didn't he wear boots?" Little Jim wanted to know. Wearing boots was one of the most important things a boy could do in the wintertime.

"Maybe his parents were poor," Poetry squawked.

"His feet are too big for him to have any parents," Dragonfly said.

And they certainly were big, as though maybe the person was a very big man, which he probably was or he wouldn't have been big enough to have knocked the living daylights out of me.

Right away, with Big Jim and Circus leading, we were on the way. Poetry and Dragonfly were next, with Little Jim and I following along behind. Little Tom Till was the only member of the gang who wasn't with us, because his parents hardly ever let him come. It was Little Tom Till's big brother, Bob, who was Big Jim's worst enemy.

We followed those shoe tracks fast and were panting and running and stopping to study them to find out which way they were going. Already they were partly covered with the fast-falling snow, so we had to hurry.

Suddenly Big Jim stopped and yelled to all of us, "Looks like he's going right straight for the Sugar Creek bridge."

It looked as if Big Jim was right, which he nearly always is, because that was the direction the tracks were going, which meant maybe that they were made by somebody who lived on the other side of the creek.

Soon we reached the bridge ourselves, and right there the tracks stopped.

"They've stopped," Big Jim said, holding my dad's flashlight close down to the ground and turning it here and there, over the bridge, along the road, into both ditches, and all around.

We all made a dive toward where Big Jim stood looking at the very last tracks, but he ordered us back. "Get back! You'll cover up any tracks if there are any!"

"But there's been a car along the road here," Poetry squawked.

Dragonfly piped up then. "I heard a car go rattling across the bridge a little while ago."

We stared at each other for a while. We knew that—with the shoe tracks disappearing and the car tracks being there—the guy had probably jumped into a car and was far away by that time with the letter and the suitcase.

Big Jim made us stand still and keep quiet for a few minutes, while he and Circus took my dad's big flashlight and walked around all over the road and along the ditches looking for tracks. Round and round they went, while the snow was falling on them and on us and quickly covering up any tracks if any had been made, and it looked as if there weren't.

All the time Big Jim and Circus were looking, I stood still, which was the hardest thing I'd had to do for a long time. I kept thinking about the pretty little brown suitcase, which my parents had bought for me, and that it was very expensive luggage. Also I kept thinking about the new pajamas and Poetry's mom's brooch and worrying, *What if we don't ever find it again?*

Then Little Jim sidled up to me. I knew he must have been thinking for quite a while—he was the only one of the Sugar Creek Gang who thought important things all by himself—because he whispered, "I'll bet it'll be easier to get him to be a Christian now than it was."

"Get who to become a Christian?" I asked.

"The thief," he said. "Now that he's stolen and done something kind of big to be sorry for, maybe it won't take God so long to show him he is a sinner and needs to be saved."

Little Jim probably didn't even know he was saying something very important, which any minister might be proud to even think of. Imagine a little guy like Little Jim being able to think of a thing like that! I knew he'd probably heard his mom or his dad say something like that at home, because it sounded like things I'd heard his pretty mom say before. His mom was a great Christian as well as being the pianist in our church and a music teacher.

After what seemed a terribly long time to have to keep still, Big Jim straightened up from looking for tracks. He sort of shrugged his shoulders and swung the flashlight around toward the sky and said, "I give up. We've lost him. He's probably a lot of miles from here in that car by now."

We all just stared at each other with serious faces, and for a minute not a one of us said a thing to anyone else. Then Dragonfly, instead of talking, got a funny look on his face all of a sudden and started to blink his eyes and to open his mouth. He is always doing that because of his being what is called allergic to nearly everything. He sneezes at almost every-thing he's never smelled before and also at nearly everything else. Then he let out a half-smothered sneeze.

"You've got a cold," Little Jim said to him.

"It's not a cold!" Dragonfly pulled a big red handkerchief out of his coat pocket, which looked as if it had maybe another bandanna or two stuffed in it for emergency in case Dragon-fly might need more than one. "It's Bill's crazy new pajamas. I smell 'em. I never could stand the smell of moth balls."

"They've been washed," I said. "Besides, they aren't here."

Dragonfly said, "I thought you said they're new."

Well, they were new, but my mom always washed new pajamas at our house before she'd let Dad or me wear them. She wanted to be sure they were sanitary after maybe being han-dled by so many people in the factory and the store.

I didn't want to be bothered with an argu-ment, so I said half-disgustedly to Dragonfly, "You wouldn't understand," which he wouldn't because his mom doesn't worry about germs the way my mom does.

Then Dragonfly sneezed again. "It's a horse. I smell a horse."

I was just getting ready to tell him, "What of it?" when behind us somewhere we heard a strange rumbling like the noise horses make when *they* sneeze, and I knew Dragonfly was right.

And Poetry, who is mischievous even at the most serious times, exclaimed, "Sure it's a horse. Hear him sneeze! He's allergic to Dragonfly!"

Big Jim whirled the flashlight in the direction of the horse's sneeze.

Then suddenly we were hit full in the face with a powerful light from somebody else's flashlight, and a man's big voice called, "Hello!" And the voice sounded like somebody's voice I'd heard before.

Whoever he was, he turned the flashlight off.

Then Big Jim shot a long beam from Dad's flashlight in the direction of the voice, and we all saw it at once. There was a big beautiful saddle horse with a man on it, and the rider was wearing a brown leather jacket and boots and looked like riders do who ride in parades on the Fourth of July.

"Did you boys want to see me?" the big gruff voice said.

Right away I got a weird feeling in my throat and in my mind, because I knew whose voice it was. It was the voice of our new man teacher at the Sugar Creek School, whom we boys had caused so much trouble for that day, and we shouldn't have.

All of a sudden I was remembering all the things that we'd done and shouldn't have. Also I remembered something I had done that I hadn't done on purpose. I was throwing a snowball at Shorty Long and accidentally hit Mr. Black on the top of his head while he was stooped over adjusting the doormat.

Of course, he hadn't been a perfect teacher, either. He had made a mistake that day when he punished me instead of Shorty Long, but that was because of his getting our names mixed up. But I knew he thought we were all a pretty bad gang of boys, which we weren't most of the time.

Then his horse started acting especially frisky, as though he wanted to get started in some direction or other. He was prancing and turning this way and that, as if it didn't make any difference which direction he went just so he could get started. And then he *did* get started, and it was right toward us. I could hear the horse's feet coming, and so could the rest of the gang.

I tell you, when it is dark like that and you hear a big horse coming in your direction very fast—and also hear a man's voice saying excitedly, "Whoa!" two or three times as though his horse is about to run away—you really want to get out of the way. We all scrambled into the ditch at the end of the bridge. We were ready to dive under it where we knew no horse could come.

We didn't get out of the way any quicker than we should have, either. We might have been trampled, because Mr. Black was having a hard time controlling his horse and was yelling excitedly, "Whoa! Steady, Prince! Whoa!"

But it wasn't doing any good. It sounded the way it does when a man's horse is being disobedient and is also scared and trying to run away. And sure enough, that was what was happening. We heard more excited whoas and more and fiercer stamping of the horse's feet. And then the horse was on the bridge, and I heard Mr. Black say, "All right then, you scared fool! Run, if you want to!"

And did that horse run! His four feet on that wooden bridge above us sounded like maybe a thousand horses' feet. He went galloping across at what my dad would have called breakneck speed, which is terribly fast. Then the horse was across the bridge, and we heard his hoofs on the road on the other side, running *gallopety-sizzle-gallop-gallop-gallop* up that road, getting farther and farther away every second.

4

Well, that was that. We'd probably made our teacher as mad as a hornet, because we had likely scared his horse. He would have it in for us tomorrow, and there would be more trouble than ever.

We'd had many a gang meeting on an old log under that end of the bridge, so we decided to stoop down and go under and have a quick meeting right then, though we wouldn't have time to sit down very long. But we'd lost the trail of whoever it was who had stolen my suitcase and the letter and Poetry's mom's brooch, and we had to decide what to do next.

So in a flash there we were, out of the falling snow and under the bridge, all of us sitting on two logs facing each other. One of the logs was a big square one, which had been left there by the men who had made the bridge. The log had too many knots in its wood to be safe to use in a bridge.

Big Jim was saving the battery in Dad's flashlight, so we just had Poetry's lantern to see each other by. It had been smoking a little and had black soot at the top of its glass globe.

It was what Dragonfly said that got us started talking about Mr. Black, our teacher, again. We were all pretty worked up because of what had happened in school on our very first day after our Christmas vacation. It wasn't easy to have to have a new teacher right in the middle of the winter—especially after we'd had such a nice pretty, kind woman teacher all the first half of the year.

"I still wish Miss Brown hadn't resigned. I'd rather have her for our teacher any time than—"

Big Jim interrupted Dragonfly by clearing his throat real loud just before he said, "But she did. And we all have to make the best of it."

"The worst of it, you mean," Dragonfly said. What he said made most of us half giggle and also grunt as though we were disgusted.

"Where do you suppose he got that pretty saddle horse?" Circus said. "I wish I had a saddle like that. Did you see those stirrups? They were gold!"

"Yeah," Poetry said, "and his spurs looked like they were solid gold too."

"What do you s'pose he was doing out on horseback?" Circus asked.

"That's what I'd like to know," Dragonfly said.

"Maybe he's out getting his exercise," Big Jim guessed. "He's from the city, you know, and lots of guys from the city ride horseback for exercise."

"Looks like the horse was getting all the exercise," Dragonfly said. He was more disgusted with Mr. Black than some of the rest of us because he had had more trouble that day than any of the rest of us, except for me.

Well, we couldn't waste any more time talking about that kind of trouble. I felt pretty terrible because of having lost my suitcase and what was in it as well as the letter. I was getting ready to say something, when Poetry spoke up.

"What are we going to do tomorrow if he doesn't behave like a good schoolteacher ought to?"

"You mean, what will he do if we don't behave like good little boys ought to?" Dragonfly said sarcastically.

"He certainly thinks we are a bunch of roughnecks," Big Jim said, and in the light of Poetry's lantern his face was pretty grim. "I think our best plan is to prove to him that we are not. After all, he is our teacher, and it's up to us to be respectful to him."

Then we took a vote and decided that we should try to be good the next day, if we could. Dragonfly was the only one to vote no. But the motion carried, and we knew he'd try to behave himself too.

"He's too suspicious of us," Dragonfly said and sneezed again. "He acts like he thinks he can't trust a one of us. And besides, I'm allergic to him."

Big Jim said something then that was kind of a bright remark. He said, "Nearly all boys are allergic to behaving themselves in school."

And Poetry spoke up and said, "Except Dragonfly. He thinks a new teacher is nothing to be sneezed at." Which was not very funny.

But we had voted to try to behave ourselves

the next day, even though I knew it wouldn't be easy. I had a very stubborn feeling in my mind, which shouldn't have been there. But it was, and I knew nearly all of us felt the same way. When a boy is good just because he *has* to be, he isn't very good.

Dragonfly all of a sudden said, "*Psst!* I hear something!"

And whenever Dragonfly hears or sees or smells something, there is nearly always something to hear or see or smell.

The silence was pretty tense for a minute while we all listened, expecting to hear most anything. Then as plain as daylight, I heard a noise from up the hill. It sounded like somebody's shoes in the snow, walking stealthily as if he was trying not to be heard.

I could feel my hair trying to stand up on end under my cap, and I looked quick at Little Jim, who was sitting close to Big Jim. His mouselike face was kind of pale. His lips were pressed together tight, and he was holding onto his stick, which was about the size of a man's cane, as tight as anything.

Big Jim had my dad's flashlight poised and pointed in the direction where we thought the sound had come from, but he hadn't turned it on yet. Poetry had the lantern sitting on his knees and was wiping some of the snow off the little ledge that ran around the bottom of it. Circus and Dragonfly were on the same log I was on, so I couldn't see what their faces looked like or guess what they were thinking. We were certainly a quiet gang for a change. I couldn't hear a thing. There wasn't a sound at all.

Big Jim whispered then, "Must have been a limb falling in the woods."

Dead limbs nearly always fall from trees in the wintertime.

Or it might have been some wild animal, I thought. There were lots of raccoons, possums, skunks, and other furbearing animals that run around in the woods along Sugar Creek at night. Once there had been a bear, and we had killed it ourselves. That is, Little Jim had, with Big Jim's rifle—but that's another story you probably know about.

Big Jim had one finger up, meaning *Keep on keeping still, everybody*—which we did. I did notice Dragonfly nervously fumbling in his coat pocket for his handkerchief, and I knew he probably had smelled something.

"Ker-chew!" went Dragonfly, reminding me of the story of Peter Rabbit, which we had in our schoolbooks when we were little. Peter Rabbit was running away from the gardener and had jumped into a big can to hide. While he was there, he had to sneeze. Then the gardener was after him again.

The very second Dragonfly sneezed, not having time to get his handkerchief out of his pocket in time to even muffle it a little bit, we heard something snap. It was just to the left of us, about twenty feet along the edge of the steep hill that dropped almost straight down from the woods above to Sugar Creek below.

Then there was a strange squeaking and something that sounded like the rattling of a chain and a thrashing around.

Then, as quick almost as we had heard it, Dragonfly smelled it. In fact we all smelled it at the same time, and we knew what it was.

"It's a skunk!" Dragonfly said. "I'm allergic to skunks!"

We all were.

You should have seen Circus come to life. His dad, as you know, was a hunter and was always catching skunks and raccoons and possums and muskrats in the wintertime to help make a living for his large family of all girls except his one boy, Circus. "My dad has a trap set in the old woodchuck den over there," he said.

Circus acted as if he'd forgotten we were having a very important meeting to decide what to do about whoever had stolen my suitcase and the letter. He reached for my dad's flashlight, which was in Big Jim's hand and which Big Jim let him have, and as quick as a flash Circus had the flashlight turned on in the direction of the sound and the smell.

And then we all saw it at the same time, something black-and-white, right at the mouth of the old woodchuck den we all knew about. The gang knew where every woodchuck den was along Sugar Creek and also every den all over the whole Sugar Creek territory.

Well, it was that skunk getting caught in Circus's dad's trap that started us on the trail of the thief again. I guess we'd all really decided that whoever he was had climbed into the car and gone across the bridge and was maybe a dozen miles away right that minute. So we certainly were surprised when we saw his tracks again, and we certainly were glad, even though we were scared too. Anyway we found the trail again right after Circus had done what he did.

Circus got to his feet and, with the flashlight in his hand, turned to Little Jim and said, "Here, give me your stick. I'll kill it so it won't have to suffer in the trap."

But Little Jim held onto his stick, saying, "No," real stubbornly. "Whyn't we let it loose instead of killing it?" he asked.

And Dragonfly said, "'Cause it's worth eight dollars, and because Circus's sisters have to have some new dresses."

"New dresses made out of skunk fur?" Poetry squawked.

"Goose!" I said. "He sells the skunk's fur to a furrier and buys the dresses with the money."

"Let me have it!" Circus said to Little Jim. "You don't want it to suffer, do you? It probably got its foot or leg broken in the trap. If we leave it till morning when Dad comes, it'll suffer all night and—"

Little Jim never could stand to see anything be hurt so he let Circus have the stick, which was a pretty ash stick, with the bark peeled off in strips around it, making it look like a big long piece of stick candy.

Anyway, that broke up our meeting, and

most of the gang followed Circus partway to where he was going, all except for Little Jim and me. Little Jim didn't want to see or hear the skunk being killed, so he held his hands over his ears to keep from hearing the sound when Circus helped it die.

It only took a minute before it was all over, and then you should have heard what happened right after that. Circus and Big Jim and Poetry and Dragonfly called Little Jim and me. They said, "Hey, Bill! Little Jim! Come quick! We've found the trail again. He's going straight toward the old sycamore tree and the cave! Hurry up!"

And that's what it looked like the thief was doing. There were tracks partly covered with the new fallen snow, leading away from the woodchuck den right up the side of the steep hill and along the ridge above Sugar Creek in the direction of the old sycamore tree.

Well, we knew that the sycamore marked the entrance to the Sugar Creek cave and that its other end was way back up in the hills in the basement of Old Man Paddler's cabin. We still had plenty of time to get to that kind old man's place before seven o'clock.

Little Jim had his stick again and was shoving it in and out of snowdrifts, trying to get the skunk "perfume" off of it so that, when he got home that night, his parents would let him take it in the house with him instead of having to leave it outside in their woodshed. Little Jim certainly was proud of that stick, and it was

46

almost as good a friend as a dog would have been. Nearly every boy needs a stick or a dog or a slingshot to keep him company.

We hadn't walked more than about a hundred yards toward the old sycamore tree when Big Jim and Circus, who were leading the way, swerved to the left a little, away from the creek, and headed out through the woods toward Bumblebee Hill. That's where the gang had so many meetings in the summertime and also where there were strawberries. We'd licked a tough town gang once in a fierce fight there. Big Jim had licked Big Bob Till in that fight, and I'd licked the daylights out of little red-headed Tom Till. Big Bob certainly was a roughneck, and we were glad *he* didn't live in Sugar Creek anymore.

The Till boys' dad was a terribly mean person, too, and also a drunkard, but he was in jail. Little Tom was a great little guy and had joined our gang. He came to our Sunday school, which it takes a brave boy to do when his brother and his father almost hate God.

It seemed the Sugar Creek Gang always had some mean person to cause them trouble. Now it was Shorty Long and his dad. I was sure it was Shorty Long's dad whose tracks we were following right that minute, because of the letter I'd had from him.

Little Jim and I were still together, so I said to him, "If ever a guy ought to be beat up on, that guy should for stealing my letter and the suitcase and—"

Little Jim surprised me by saying, "Let's don't beat up on him. Let's be kind to him. My mom is trying to get his mom saved. His dad is terribly mean to her and—"

"I don't think it was Shorty," I said. "I think it was his dad!"

Whoever it was we were trailing must have changed his mind about being in a hurry the way he was before, for now he didn't walk close to an oak or a cedar or fir or pine tree to hide his tracks but stayed out in the open.

"He wants the falling snow to cover his tracks," Big Jim said and called us to hurry up. "See here—you can't even see the hole in his shoe sole anymore."

"He's quit running, though," Circus said. "He must not be scared."

"They look like *boot* tracks to me," Poetry said, when he dropped back beside Little Jim and me. He was having a hard time to keep up with the rest of us because of having to carry so much more weight than anyone else.

At the foot of Bumblebee Hill we passed the tree where Little Jim had killed the bear, and we started following the tracks up the hill. There was an old abandoned cemetery up there where Old Man Paddler's wife was buried, and there were a lot of very old weather-beaten, old-fashioned tombstones. Old Man Paddler's wife's tombstone was the only new one in the whole cemetery.

Pretty soon we were up there, and the tracks led right past her tall stone.

Big Jim flashed his light on it for a minute, and we all saw the sculptured hand on it that had one finger pointing toward the sky. We saw the words right below it, which said *"There Is Rest in Heaven."*

Old Man Paddler had had that carved on it during the past summer. Some other smaller tombstones were there too, which had the names of Old Man Paddler's boys on them.

Then I let out a yell and said, "Hey, what in the—"

One of my boots had stepped into a woodchuck hole, and I had gone all the way down to my knee. I remembered then that there were about a half-dozen woodchuck dens around there. I had accidentally stepped into one. Not only that, but the minute I stepped in, I felt something shut tight on my boot! I knew it must be another one of Circus's dad's traps, which he had set in nearly every woodchuck den in the territory.

But the gang didn't pay any attention to me, because there was more excitement up ahead. So I got out of the den and the trap as quickly as I could and joined them.

There were a lot of half-covered snow tracks, and just outside another hole was a steel trap with its jaws closed. Nothing was in it except some long gray hairs, which looked like a possum's fur, and also there was some blood.

All of a sudden we all straightened up and looked at each other.

"Your dad!" I said to Circus. "We're on the

wrong trail. It's your dad's tracks. He's running his trapline tonight."

"He is not," Circus said. "He's not at home. He—what—"

Circus's fists doubled up, and I could see his jaw set. He held Poetry's lantern close to the thrown trap and studied the whitish-gray fur caught in its jaws.

Somehow I felt that he was going to say something very important, which he did. He said, "Whoever he is, he not only stole Bill's suitcase, but he is a poacher. He's been running my dad's trapline and taking out anything that's been caught. The—why, the—the dirty—"

Then Circus raised his voice and cried to us, "Come on, gang, let's hurry up and trail him. Dad's been telling us he *thought* somebody was poaching, and now we know! We know!"

5

Now there were three of us who'd had something stolen by the guy, whoever he was, and not a one of us knew who.

"I'll bet it *is* Shorty Long's dad," Circus said over his shoulder to Little Jim and me, who were still the last ones because Little Jim had the shortest legs of any of us and couldn't keep up.

"What makes you think so?" Big Jim asked when he heard Circus say that.

"Because Pop began to miss things out of his traps about the same time Shorty's family moved into the neighborhood. And nearly every time something had been stolen, it seemed like it was after a snowstorm when the tracks would be covered up, the way they are tonight. Boy, oh, boy, I'd hate to think what would happen if Pop would ever catch him at it. It'd be just too bad."

We were walking fast, following those half-covered tracks, going back toward the cave at the sycamore tree again, because there, not far from the swamp, Circus's dad had several muskrat traps set.

Pretty soon, while we were puffing along, panting and dodging bushes and trees and briars and brush piles, getting closer and closer to the swamp, we suddenly stopped. I bumped right square into Poetry, who was in front of me. He had stopped because Circus and Big Jim had stopped first, and I heard Big Jim say under his breath, "*Sh!* Quiet!"

As quick as a flash, Circus, who had been carrying Poetry's lantern, swung around toward us, holding the lantern up close to his face as though he was going to study it to see if it was all right. Then he pressed down on the little control lever that lifts the globe. He gave a fierce, quick blow, and out went the light. Also I noticed that Big Jim had turned off my dad's flashlight, and not a one of us could see anyone else. It was pitch-dark, although the snow everywhere on the ground made it light enough so we could see that we were all there. But we looked like nothing but shadows.

"'S'matter?" I said.

Big Jim shushed us all again. And it was a rule in our gang that when Big Jim shushed us, we all shushed as best we could.

Then Big Jim said in a husky whisper, "Look, gang. Right over there at the edge of the swamp. See?"

There *was* something. About twenty feet off the side of the path that goes through the swamp, and not very far from the mouth of the cave, there was a light. Somebody was stooped over and doing something, but we couldn't see what at first.

We could see *him*, but with our lights out he couldn't see us at all, we were sure.

We all huddled close together when Big Jim told us to, so that we could hear what he was going to tell us.

I had a feeling that there was going to be some excitement again, like the kind we had had before at this very place. In fact, the man with the light was almost at the very same spot where we had once caught a bank robber a long time ago. It was also close to the place where Old Man Paddler had had his money buried under a swamp rosebush. We were sort of used to running into all kinds of mysteries and having fights and catching robbers and things, but I was always trembling inside every time we bumped into another exciting adventure.

Now that our eyes were getting more used to the darkness, I could see a little better. I could see that the man had a lantern that was shining on something he was doing. I couldn't see very well, but—the way it looked to me— the lantern was probably standing on the ground behind a log. He was sitting on the log himself, and I couldn't guess what he was doing.

But Circus seemed to know. He whispered, "It was maybe too big a possum to carry, so he's skinning it and will throw the carcass over in the swamp. Then he'll just carry the pelt, which won't be very heavy." A pelt was an undressed fur skin.

"You kids stay here," Big Jim ordered most of us, "and Circus and I'll sneak up and see if that's what he is doing. We've got to know if he's the one who's been stealing from Circus's dad's traps."

"How about my suitcase and the letter?" I said. "Find out if it's Shorty Long's dad."

I didn't think it was fair for Circus and Big Jim to get to go without the rest of us, especially me, because I was still mad. And I could just imagine myself sneaking up on whoever it was and then, when Big Jim gave the signal, all of us diving in headfirst and grabbing him and getting him down and sitting on him and being heroes the way we had been when we caught the robber.

But there wasn't any use for me to wish it.

"All you guys have got to do is to keep still," Big Jim ordered us under his breath. "We'll sneak around on the other side of him, come up from behind the big fir tree, and find out who it is."

"Then what?" I asked.

"That's enough to know now," Big Jim whispered back. "I don't know yet myself."

It didn't help matters any for Big Jim to say that. In fact, when he said he didn't know himself, that started my mind off to thinking and planning and scheming what we'd better do.

It was certainly hard to keep still. I could see Circus and Big Jim's shadows as they moved off to the right, getting ready to make a wide circle around the man on the log. Pretty soon they got too far for us to see in the falling snow, and all we could do was wait, and keep still, and feel weird inside every time we heard a noise that sounded like Circus or Big Jim stepping on a stick that snapped or stumbling over something.

Little Jim was holding onto my arm with his mittened hands. I could still smell the skunk a little on his stick, but not much.

It felt good to have Little Jim snuggle up close to me, because I was bigger than he was and I thought maybe it made him feel braver to be there. It also made *me* feel braver when I thought that maybe he felt braver because of me. And while I was thinking that, I felt as if I could lick anybody, anywhere, any size, just to protect Little Jim from getting hurt. He was such a great little guy. My dad is always thinking important things and, as I've already told you, knows the Bible real well. He told me one day, "Having Little Jim in the Sugar Creek Gang helps give the gang a conscience."

I couldn't understand what Dad meant, and I still don't very well. But he explained that Little Jim is always there to tell the gang when they are about to do something they shouldn't. And after the gang has done something wrong, Little Jim feels terribly sad, just like your conscience when you do wrong.

I knew Dad was right, as he usually is, even though I don't always understand.

Anyway right that minute, while Big Jim and Circus were creeping around and up on that guy on the log, and while Poetry and Dragonfly and Little Jim and I were waiting, and while Little Jim was holding onto my arm, I began to feel just a little bit sorry for the man, whoever he was, because he was going to have to get beat up on by all of us.

"Sh!" Poetry whispered. "Look! He's drinking something out of a bottle!"

We looked, and that is what it looked like— a big bottle of something flashed in the light of his lantern for a second.

"Maybe it's his lunch. Maybe he's drinking out of his thermos bottle," Little Jim said, which shows he never liked to think bad things about people if he could help it. He'd rather think a guy was drinking milk or cocoa or coffee out of a thermos than that he was drinking whiskey.

Then Dragonfly said something that made me feel sad.

"Maybe it is Circus's pop. Maybe he decided to come home and run his traplines tonight before the snow covers everything up. Maybe that's him on the log skinning his own possum, and maybe he's drinking whiskey again."

"Absolutely not," I said, angry. "Circus's dad was converted, wasn't he? Didn't he get saved in those evangelistic meetings? How could he get drunk if he is a Christian?"

"He might backslide," Poetry said.

"What's that?" Dragonfly asked, knowing less than most any of the gang about the Bible.

"That's when a person who has become a Christian turns his back on the church—and— and—on the Lord and gets bad again," Little Jim said.

We didn't have time to whisper anything else, because just then we heard a noise up there ahead of us. The man on the log looked up, grabbed his lantern, jumped to his feet, and started to run in our direction. The first thing he did, though, was to stumble over the log and fall down, get up quick and awkward-like, and start right toward us again.

We heard Big Jim and Circus yelling on the other side of him, "Stop, thief! Hey, gang! Bill! Poetry! Stop him!"

Well, there the four of us littlest guys were, without either Big Jim or Circus to help us, and the man, whoever he was, was running in our direction, waving his lantern in front of him to see his way and stumbling along as though he was drunk toward the fir tree behind which we were hiding.

I guessed what he was going to try to do. He was going to make a dive for the mouth of the cave, which was just about fifty feet to the left of us, and in order to get to it he would have to pass the fir tree where we were.

I don't know how I ever managed to think straight, but I must have, because I heard myself saying to the guys with me, "Wait'll he gets here, and then all four of us dive out and tackle him football style."

Boy, oh, boy, I certainly couldn't think straight, but it suddenly seemed, with Big Jim and Circus gone, that I was the leader of our little gang. So I felt very brave, in spite of being scared, and was all set to be the first one to grab the man when he got to where we were.

But I didn't even have a chance to be a hero—not the first one, anyway. We were all crouched there waiting when, all of a sudden, as the man got close enough, Little Jim shot out from beside me and shoved his stick right between the man's flying legs.

Ker-whamety-squash-squash-flop. The guy fell right in front of us in a tangled-up sprawl. His lantern flew out of his hand as he tried to catch himself, and in an instant we were all on top of him. Big Jim and Circus got there in a split second.

It didn't take long for all of us to be right in the middle of one of the fiercest wrestling fights we'd ever had—at least the fiercest one we'd had for a long time. Not since the fight we'd had in this same place about a year ago, when we caught the bank robber, had I heard so much swearing and grunting and groaning as I heard right that minute. Even while I was holding on like a bulldog to the man's right leg, Circus was holding onto his other leg, and Poetry and Big Jim and Little Jim and Dragonfly were tumbling all over him and getting socked by the man's fists every now and then before we could get him under control.

Even while we were doing all that, I was sorry that Little Jim had to be there; because, honestly, I'd never heard a man swear so much in my life. The words that came out of his mouth were actually worse to hear than the mud in our barnyard looks in the spring when the ground has begun to thaw out after a long winter.

The swearing was terrible, and if there is anything Little Jim can't stand more than anything else it is to hear somebody swear. Little Jim not only knows it is wrong to swear, but he has a special reverence for the Bible and for the One who is the main character in it.

It didn't take us long to get that guy down, all of us sitting and half lying on his legs and arms and on him himself. I hadn't even had time to decide who he was. Of course, I couldn't see his face, but I'd heard his voice and the swear words, and it was the voice of somebody who lived in the Sugar Creek neighborhood, I was sure, because I'd heard that voice before a good many times. In fact it seemed that every time I'd heard it before, it had been swearing.

All of a sudden, Dragonfly, panting for breath even worse than he sometimes does when he is in a fight, said, "It's—it's—hey, gang! It's John Till! He's out of jail again!"

And that was who it was. I knew it the minute Dragonfly said it, and it made what we were doing seem terribly important. The last any of us had seen of old John Till, he had been on the way to jail. Boy, oh, boy, oh, boy! Here we were catching a jailbird just as if we were real detectives or the FBI or somebody else important! It surely felt good, even though the snowdrift we had caught him in was pretty cold and didn't feel like anybody's nice, big, soft, warm featherbed.

For some reason, though, I wasn't very glad. Maybe it was because I knew that John Till was Little Tom Till's dad, and Little Tom was a great little guy, who had joined our gang and even came to our Sunday school. But the man was Big Bob Till's dad too. And as you already know, Big Bob was a real tough guy and Big Jim's worst enemy and was always causing the gang trouble when he used to live in our neighborhood.

The first time I'd ever seen John Till was one summer when he was working in my dad's oat field and had tried to give Circus's dad some whiskey to drink. That very day Circus and I had had a fight with him. I'd had the living daylights knocked out of me right in the middle of the fight too, or rather at the end of it, because for some reason the fight didn't last very long after I got licked.

And then we heard a high-pitched, quavering old voice saying from behind us somewhere, "Hello, boys! What's going on here? What are you doing out here in the snow?"

Even before I could think, I knew who it was, and something inside of me just bubbled up with happiness. It was the voice of the kindest old man in the world, long-whiskered Old Man Paddler himself, the best grown-up friend the Sugar Creek Gang ever had. I knew that he had just come out of the mouth of the cave by the sycamore tree, because the other end of the long cave came out in the basement of his cabin way up in the hills. He'd probably got tired waiting for us to come and had decided to come to the mouth of the cave to wait for us. Maybe it was way past time for us to meet him as we were supposed to at seven o'clock.

I looked up at him. He was carrying an old-fashioned kerosene lantern that had a shield at the back so that the light came out just at the front and sides. His whiskers were as white as the snow itself and reached down to the place where his belt probably was. He had on a coat and probably wore suspenders, which old men nearly always do.

He was wearing his thick-lensed glasses, I noticed, and had a cane hanging in the crook of his arm, and in his hand was something that looked like—like a—why it *was!* It was my *little brown suitcase!*

Before I could cry out to the gang and tell them what I'd seen, the old man said, "Mighty nice of you boys to come to meet me. I was afraid I couldn't go because I might get lost at night. I don't see so very well at night anymore. Why—what's that? Is somebody hurt?"

It was old hook-nosed John Till, gasping and saying, "Let me up, you little roughnecks! Get off of me. Get off!"

6

When I looked up and saw that kind old man with his gray-brown raccoonskin cap on his fine head with its high forehead and the smile that I could imagine he had on his face— I wasn't able to see his smile because of his whiskers—I had a sort of guilty feeling as if I had either done something wrong or else was doing it right that minute.

That old man hates wickedness worse than anything. He loves our wonderful country and is very patriotic and wants everybody to obey the law. He is always wishing nobody made or sold liquor of any kind, especially whiskey, because it spoils so many lives and breaks so many hearts. Yet I knew that he wouldn't want us to hurt old John Till but would rather we would be kind to him.

There were so many things to think about right that second, and I didn't have time to think about a one of them. There was Mr. Black, our teacher, who had galloped away on his horse and who would maybe have it in for the whole gang of us the next day at school. There in Old Man Paddler's hand was my little brown suitcase, which had my pajamas in it and, I hoped, Poetry's mom's beautiful new brooch, which she had left at our house. There was the letter, which somebody had stolen from me and which had said that I was a roughneck and that the whole Sugar Creek Gang was a bunch of roughnecks. And there was the wrestling fight we had been having with old John Till, whose leg I still was holding onto. So I didn't have time to think about much of anything.

Also I knew we probably ought to get going with Old Man Paddler to Poetry's house, where all our parents were waiting for us and wondering what on earth had happened to us.

Right that minute John Till started squirming and kicking, or rather trying to, and twisting and grunting and swearing and calling us names. His voice was pretty muffled, because he was down on his stomach, and his face was probably mixed up in snow.

The gang was grunting, too, I tell you.

Circus must have felt as I did about what Old Man Paddler would maybe think we were doing and shouldn't have been, because he said to the old man from between his gritted teeth, "He's been stealing my dad's fur from his traps, and we caught him at it. He was skinning a possum which he took out of a trap up on Bumblebee hill!"

Poetry piped up. "He stole my mother's beautiful new brooch."

And I chimed in between grunts, "And my suitcase and a letter, and he called us a bunch of roughnecks!"

John Till let out a roar, made a mighty

heave of his body, shoved out his arms, and tried to push us all off. But he couldn't, so he yelled, "I did not. You're a bunch of liars! Let me up, I tell you, or I'll—I'll—"

Whatever it was he wanted to do to us, we knew he wouldn't get a chance to do it unless we gave him a chance, and we weren't going to do that, no sir!

Big Jim, who was sprawled across John Till's shoulders, holding him down with all his strength, cut in then and said fiercely, "John Till! We're not letting you up! Understand? We're going to tie your hands behind you, and you're going to walk along with us until we get to Poetry's house. Then we're taking you in somebody's car to town and back to jail."

John Till let out a couple of fierce swear words and said, "You're not taking me to anybody's jail. I've been in jail enough in my life!"

"You *are* going to jail!" Big Jim said to him through his teeth. "We caught you stealing out of Circus's dad's traps, and that's where you're going!"

Well, I don't know what we would have done with John Till if Old Man Paddler's kind voice hadn't broken in then and said, "Listen, boys, listen!"

For a minute everything was quiet, and I had a feeling that the old man was going to say something very important. He was sort of like my dad, always saying things that were different. Since he was a good Christian and lived like one all the time, I knew he would maybe say something about the Bible. And sure enough, he did. It made me wish I could think of things like that instead of always wanting to beat up on somebody.

Anyway, this is what that kind, quavering, high-pitched old voice said: "He deserves punishment, boys, but he doesn't need to be punished nearly so much as he needs to be changed. He needs to hear the gospel, and maybe he needs somebody to be kind to him."

Then Old Man Paddler changed his tone of voice and talked straight to John Till himself. All of us, including John Till, kept quiet to listen.

This is what the old man said—and, wow, did he say it like he meant business, even though he used a kind voice: "John Till, you are out on parole. If I hadn't believed you'd go straight, I wouldn't have let them parole you to me. But I did believe it, and—"

Even while Old Man Paddler was "talking turkey" to John Till, who had to listen whether he wanted to or not, I thought about what a kind person that old man really was. Imagine his going to the jail or to the judge or wherever he had gone and asking them to let John Till out and to parole him over to him! It certainly showed that Old Man Paddler wasn't always thinking about himself. Right then he was telling John Till things that maybe his own dad should have told him a long time ago, so he wouldn't have grown up to be such a wicked man.

Old Man Paddler was saying, "For the sake of your wife and your two boys, Bob and Tom, and for your own sake, John, you've got to go straight this time. If you have to go back to jail, it'll mean a longer sentence and probably the state penitentiary for you. Then who'll look after your family? Who'll buy the groceries and clothes and shoes? No, John, now's the time to go straight! You don't have to steal to get money either. There's plenty of work for you right here in Sugar Creek territory."

And John Till just sort of melted under the old man's words like a chunk of ice would melt in a fire.

Then Old Man Paddler finished talking to John Till and said to all of us, "You can let him up, boys! We'll take him along with us to the Thompsons'."

And pretty soon all of us were up and knocking the snow off each other, looking around to see if any of us had lost anything, and getting ready to get going to Poetry's house.

The first thing I did was to get my suitcase from Old Man Paddler and open it to see if everything was in it and was all right, and it was.

"Where in the world did you find it?" I asked him.

"It was just inside the cave. I almost stumbled over it when I came out," he said. "Some of you boys planning to stay at my cabin all night?"

Dragonfly piped up then. "John Till stole it

from Bill—grabbed it out of his hand at the entrance to Poetry's lane—and stole a letter Bill had, and knocked the living daylights out of him, and shoved him into a snowdrift, and—"

John Till had been standing sort of in a daze, as though he was hardly there, the way drunk men do sometimes. When he heard that, he came to life and said angrily "Th-that's a lie!" And he made a lunge at Dragonfly.

Dragonfly ducked John Till's awkward fist and dived behind a tree. John, who was getting drunker every minute because of the whiskey he had drunk, stumbled over a tree root and fell down again in the snow.

"We'd better search him for the letter," Big Jim said.

Old Man Paddler let us do that. But there wasn't a letter in any of his pockets, which was hard to believe.

"I'll bet you tore it up," Dragonfly said.

John Till said, "I don't know anything about a letter."

Well, we really had to get going, and there wasn't any use to argue with a drunk man, who was getting drunker every minute.

Circus took Dad's flashlight and hurried back to the log to get the possum, which was almost half skinned. With all of us helping a little as well as talking, he finished skinning it and tossed the carcass over into the swamp.

We started right away to Poetry's house, with Circus carrying the very pretty grayish-white possum pelt draped over his arm. John

Till didn't want to go along, but Old Man Paddler said he had to. So he shuffled along with us.

"He stole that possum out of Circus's dad's trap on Bumblebee Hill," Dragonfly said to Old Man Paddler. "We caught him right in the act of skinning it. We followed his tracks all the way, so we know he took it."

And then I got the surprise of my life, for Old Man Paddler said, "The traps on Bumblebee Hill belong to John. I've just made arrangements with Dan Browne to let John trap there."

Dan Browne was Circus's dad's name. Maybe you know, too, that Old Man Paddler owned nearly all the land all around Bumblebee Hill and also the woods.

Well, John Till had denied having stolen my suitcase, and not only that, but Old Man Paddler himself said that the traps on Bumblebee Hill actually belonged to John Till himself. So things were more mixed up than ever.

But who did steal my suitcase and knock me into the middle of the snowdrift? Who was the man who had written the letter and shoved it into our mailbox? If it wasn't John Till, then it had to be Shorty Long's dad.

"It's got to be John Till or Shorty Long's dad," Dragonfly said to me, as he and Poetry and Little Jim and I walked along behind Old Man Paddler and Big Jim and Circus and John Till.

"Why?" Little Jim's mouselike voice asked,

and I could see he didn't want it to be either one of them.

"Because," Dragonfly said, "the letter you told us about said the gang had been beating up on his son, didn't it?"

"Yeah, that's right," Poetry said. "That's what Bill said it said—that it was a pity that a family can't move into a neighborhood without a gang of roughnecks beating up on his boy. And we've had fights with both Shorty Long and Bob Till, haven't we?"

"And licked both of them," Dragonfly said, and I knew he was right. We'd had fights with both Bob and Shorty, so either one of their dads could have written the letter.

Once when Little Jim and I were side by side, as we nearly always are, he said to me, "They're going to sing church hymns, and Old Man Paddler is going to give a talk out of the Bible just before everybody goes home."

"They are?" I said, and somehow I began to feel very good on the inside of me, as though I had either done something I should have or else hadn't done something I shouldn't have.

All of a sudden I had the kindest feeling for old hook-nosed John Till! I didn't even hate him. I could just see him, in my imagination, sitting with all the Sugar Creek Gang and their parents and also a few girls in Poetry's basement, with everybody singing one of our pretty church songs and Little Jim's mom playing the piano that I knew Poetry's parents had put in their recreation room.

Then I could imagine John Till sitting in a chair with the rest of the people and listening to Old Man Paddler, who would sit with his Bible open in his gnarled old hands and tell everybody something wonderful. Boy, oh, boy! John Till would *have* to listen, for if he didn't—well, he'd be scared we'd call the sheriff. It might be the first time in his life he would hear an honest-to-goodness talk from the Bible from somebody who really believed it and lived it. It certainly wouldn't hurt him any.

And then I remembered what Dad had said too—that sometimes a person needs a friend first before he becomes a Christian.

We were hurrying along as fast as we could, when all of a sudden Dragonfly said, "Listen, everybody!"

We all stopped dead still in our tracks, old John Till stopping last of all. And then we all heard it—horse's hoofs going *gallopety-sizzle* across the Sugar Creek bridge, terribly fast. We knew that our new teacher was on his way back from wherever he had been, and we wondered where he was going and why. Right away we couldn't hear him anymore—not just then anyway.

7

Soon we came to Poetry's lane, climbed over the fence, and started toward the lighted house. There were all kinds of car tracks in the lane and horse tracks also. Some of the parents probably had come in sleighs. A lot of cars were parked by the gate at Poetry's house, as well as several sleighs, and we knew our parents and probably a lot of babies and girls of the neighborhood were there already.

We really had a wonderful time in Poetry's new basement even though later on, when Mr. Black came, he made us feel that we had to be more quiet than we wanted to be.

The basement was all lighted with new electric lights—Poetry's family was the only family in our neighborhood to have their own electric generator. It certainly would be a good place for the gang to play games and do things, I thought, when I saw the green-topped Ping-Pong table and its little white net and four new paddles and balls. The dartboard hanging on the cream-colored wall had the kind of backboard so that a mother wouldn't care if your dart happened to miss the target and stick into it. Also it made me feel good when I saw the big lazy chairs to lounge in and a small radio and even the piano with songbooks on it. Poetry's accordion was on top of the piano, and there was a fireplace and floor lamps and everything. The floor was made out of some kind of different-colored asphalt tile, Poetry told me, which made the old dark basement at our house look like nothing.

For a minute I was glad Mom wasn't there, because it might start her to worrying a little bit about *our* basement. But Mom didn't worry out loud as much as she used to, because she was a better Christian than she had been before Charlotte Ann was born.

Well, it was a great neighborhood gathering. Nearly every one of the gang's parents was there, and a lot of the girls from Sugar Creek School, and also some babies who didn't know how to keep quiet and some who did.

Everybody was standing up or sitting down and talking about this or that or somebody or somebody else, and everybody was talking to everybody with nobody listening to anybody. Sitting off in a corner, looking at pictures in a magazine by a floor lamp, was John Till in his old clothes, acting as though he was bored to death with what was going on.

Little Jim's dad, who was the township trustee and always made everybody like him by being interested in them, went around from one lonesome-looking person to another, making them glad they had come. He didn't have very much luck with old John, though.

It wasn't until Little Jim was asked to play a piano solo on the program, which started pretty soon, that John Till showed any interest. Poetry and Dragonfly and I were sitting on the stairway that led up to their kitchen, at the top of which was a door leading out into their yard.

"Look!" Poetry said. "Little Tom's dad is keeping time with his feet."

Pretty soon Circus was ordered to sing a solo. First, he was *asked* by the chairman of the meeting. Then, when he didn't want to, he was *ordered* to by his mom. Since that was a rule in our gang—you had to obey your parents—Circus sang it. The song was:

> What a friend we have in Jesus,
> All our sins and griefs to bear.

John Till looked down all the time.

I was sitting there on a step with Poetry, with Dragonfly behind and above us. I could imagine that maybe John was thinking about his sins and maybe being sorry for them. And then I also was thinking about what Dad had said about some people needing to have a friend before they decided to become Christians. I thought that maybe nobody who was an honest-to-goodness Christian had ever been as kind to John Till as Old Man Paddler was and that maybe sometime that mean old drunkard would even want to have the Friend Circus was singing about.

It was when Old Man Paddler was called on to make what they called the "Dedicatory Prayer" that we heard a noise outside that sounded like a horse galloping, getting closer and closer to the house. Then, while he was making his way through the crowd up to the little desk near the fireplace, we heard a noise outside that sounded like a horse snorting. And then Dragonfly sneezed.

I knew it was Mr. Black coming late to the dedication. We were all sorry, although I wished for a moment that he had come sooner and had heard Little Jim play and Circus sing. Maybe he would have decided that we were not such a tough gang as he thought, and he might have been kinder to us the next day.

I turned around awfully quick to Dragonfly to shush him from sneezing again. That little guy really was looking miserable. For the first time I noticed a sty on his right eye, and I felt sorry for him because I'd had some sties myself.

He sneezed again three times, and I knew it was either the horse or else just the fact that Dragonfly was *thinking* about the horse. Then, just as Old Man Paddler asked everybody to stand up, Dragonfly sneezed again. This time he turned his face to one side and half smothered the sneeze in his handkerchief.

He certainly had a funny way of sneezing. First, he would half open his small mouth, and then he would grab his nose and blink his eyes several times, as if he was really going to do something important. Next, he'd take a big breath, and both eyes would shut real tight. Then out would come the silliest little sneeze you ever heard. That is, it always sounded like that if he could get hold of his nose quick enough. But if the sneeze came too quick, it sounded just like anybody's ordinary sneeze. And a teacher in a schoolhouse couldn't tell whose it was.

But this time Dragonfly's sneeze was crazier than usual. Half the people who were near us looked around to see what kind of an explosion had happened.

Dragonfly's sty had caused it. When he shut his eyes tight, as he always does, it must have hurt his sty, because right after the tail end of his funny little sneeze, he said, "Ouch!" as though I had pinched him.

I hadn't, although I wanted to. It wasn't any time to be funny—right when Old Man Paddler was getting ready to make the dedicatory prayer.

Just as the old man was about to begin to pray, there was a knock at the door right behind us at the top of the stairs. Poetry's mom looked over at us boys and nodded for one of us to open the door to let in whoever it was. I didn't want to, thinking it was Mr. Black, but I did. And that's who it was.

Everything would have been interrupted for a minute if Old Man Paddler had known somebody was coming in, but he was at the farthest end of the basement and didn't hear. So he just went right on getting ready to pray.

Most of the people bowed their heads, and the rest of them looked at the stairway to see who was coming in. Most of those who were looking were some girls from the Sugar Creek School who had been looking toward the stairway anyway because of Dragonfly's sneeze.

Well, while our teacher was coming partway down the stairs so that he could see and hear, Old Man Paddler started to pray. I was glad Mr. Black was there for that, because it was the nicest prayer I'd ever heard that kind, long-whiskered old man pray. It was all about Poetry's family and the nice basement and how it was going to be used for the right purposes and only for the glory of the Lord and things like that.

Part of the prayer, which I was especially glad Mr. Black was hearing, was "And may nothing ever be done here which will bring dishonor to Your name—nothing said or done, nothing that is worldly or unworthy of the name Christian. Bless all the boys who will play here, the boys of the Sugar Creek Gang . . ."

Then he told the Lord that we were a pretty fine gang of boys, which I also thought was good for Mr. Black to hear, even if it wasn't always true all the time. The prayer finished something like this: "And if there are any here tonight who do not know You, who are not saved, may they come to realize that the Lord Jesus Christ died for them and that they may be saved simply by turning from their sins and trusting in Him."

When the prayer was finished, Mr. Black very quietly and with very good manners came on down the steps and into the basement. He was met by Poetry's mom and dad, and everybody started to get introduced to him.

Then Poetry's dad decided it would be a good thing to introduce him to everybody at once, so he clapped his hands for attention.

And then—would you believe it?—just when everybody was so quiet you could have heard a pin drop, Dragonfly got that funny look on his face, reached for his handkerchief, blinked his eyes, shut them quick, grabbed his nose, and let out that silly little sneeze, and again he said "Ouch!"

Well, Mr. Black heard him. He looked around as quick as a flash, saw who it was, and frowned. Some of the girls giggled, and then Poetry's dad introduced Mr. Black, who made a very nice speech. But I didn't like it very well, because of not liking him very well.

Everybody clapped for him—except some of us. I looked at Poetry. Instead of clapping, he was using one hand to fan his face. Circus was looking at me and, instead of clapping, had one of his hands upside down and was spanking it, as though it was a boy getting a licking. Little Jim, who was over on the piano bench, pretty close to Mr. Black, had his two hands together and was going to clap until he saw the frown on my face. Then he just slipped his hands down onto his lap and clapped a tiny bit. Dragonfly had to hold his nose with his handkerchief and couldn't clap at all. Only Big Jim clapped, and I knew it was because he wanted to be good-mannered.

It looked like the whole gang had the same stubborn feeling I had in my mind. It was the way Mr. Black kept his eye on us all the time, as though he wondered what on earth kind of people we were, or if we were even human beings. That bothered me, and yet it seemed all the grown-up people there liked him, especially the mothers.

He really made a good speech, though. I wouldn't have time to tell you all about it—I'll only give you the first few words. He said, after they made him go up to the other end of the room to talk, "Ladies and gentlemen, parents and families of the Sugar Creek School District, I feel very much at home in this friendly gathering tonight—much more so than the Hoosier schoolmaster felt in the famous book by that name, even though my experiences on my first day of teaching have led me to think that I may have the privilege of living over in reality some of the disturbing and ludicrous experiences of that famous teacher—"

I lost out on the next few words, because Dragonfly whispered in my ear and wanted to know what "ludicrous" meant. Since I knew the word meant something ridiculous, something that would make people laugh, I said, "The way you sneeze is ludicrous."

That night, after the party was over and everybody was gone, Poetry and I were alone upstairs in his room getting ready to go to bed. I asked him, "Have you ever read any of the ludicrous experiences in the book called *The Hoosier Schoolmaster?*"

He said, "No, have you?"

"No," I answered.

"But I've got the book," he said. He slid off the edge of the bed, shuffled across the room in his flapping pajamas, and took a small book out of his library.

After we had said our prayers and climbed in, we sat up in bed for a few minutes with his bed lamp on and read a little out of the book. But what we read made us mad, because the boys in the story were a really tough gang, and the man teacher was almost a perfect angel. It made me mad to think Mr. Black would compare our gang to the actual roughnecks in that story.

"Look here!" Poetry said. "Look at this picture!"

I looked, and it was a full-paged glossy picture of a teacher upon the roof of the schoolhouse, holding a board on the top of the chimney. The door of the schoolhouse was open, and a gang of tough-looking boys was tumbling out along with a lot of smoke. The story told about how one day the boys had locked the teacher out, and he had been smarter than they were and had climbed up on the roof and put a board over the chimney. Then the stove had smoked and smoked, and the boys had to unlock the door and, choking and sputtering, had to come out.

Well, we had to go to sleep sometime. So we

sighed to each other, and Poetry turned out the light.

The next thing I knew it was morning. It was a nice day, a whole lot warmer than it was the day before, but there was a lot of trouble ahead for us all.

8

The first thing I thought about when I woke up was all the things that had happened the night before—the stolen and found-again suitcase, the fight we'd had with John Till, and the dedication of Poetry's parents' basement. As I nearly always do, I woke up sooner than I wanted to. I wanted to go right back to sleep again but couldn't, because Poetry's mom called upstairs to where we were and said to come on down to breakfast.

It was a very interesting breakfast—bacon and eggs and pancakes. First, though, we all sat very quietly behind our plates while Poetry's dad passed a little box around for each one of us to take out a small card. Each card had a Bible verse printed on it. Then each one of us took turns reading out loud what was printed on our cards.

I sort of stared at mine when I saw what it was, and for some reason I was glad my dad wasn't there to hear me read it. This is what it was: "He who spares his rod hates his son, but he who loves him disciplines him diligently [Proverbs 13:24]." I knew that meant that parents were supposed to punish their boys when they needed it, so that their boys wouldn't be spoiled and grow up to be like John Till or

Shorty Long's dad, or Bob Till, or Shorty Long himself.

When Poetry read his verse, it looked as if his parents had picked out the verses for both of us to read. But we knew they hadn't, because we had pulled them out of the middle of the box ourselves. Anyway, there it was, and Poetry's squawky voice read it without even hesitating: "Be kind to one another, tender-hearted, forgiving each other, just as God in Christ also has forgiven you [Ephesians 4:32]."

I knew right away that I was supposed to be kind to Shorty Long and to forgive him.

Poetry's mom and dad read their verses, and his dad prayed, thanking the Lord for our breakfast and also for forgiving us all our sins on account of Jesus Himself. I guess maybe I'd never thought about it that way before. But right that minute, while I had my eyes shut and while I could hear the teakettle singing on their stove and while I could smell the fried eggs and bacon—and also while I knew Poetry's mom was wondering if the pancakes were ready to be turned over—Poetry's dad said in his prayer, "And we know that the reason why You are able to forgive us at all is because Your Son, Jesus, died for us, and so our sins have all been atoned for."

Poetry's mom had to leave the table then for a second to look after the pancakes. I forgot to keep my eyes closed and watched her instead, so I missed the rest of the prayer. But I knew that God couldn't take any people to heaven just because they were good, but because of Jesus Himself. All of a sudden I felt something kind of warm inside my heart, as if I loved Somebody very much, and I was glad I was alive. He could forgive even the worst person in the world for the same reason.

Poetry's dad was kind of like my dad—not praying very long when he knew a hungry boy was waiting for his breakfast. So right away he was through, and we all talked about different things, especially what had happened the night before.

"What'll we do with all the pie and cake and sandwiches that were left over?" Poetry's dad said.

Poetry said, "I could probably manage to eat two or three of the blackberry pies, if I had to."

I said, "I could probably manage to help you."

But Poetry said, "I wouldn't think of making you."

It had been all settled the night before, though, by the different parents. Because that day was Old Man Paddler's birthday, they had decided that the Sugar Creek Gang could go up to his cabin right after school and take him a whole basketful of pie and cake and sandwiches and salads and fried chicken and stuff. We would have a picnic supper in his old clapboard-roofed cabin in front of his fireplace. Boy, oh, boy, that would be fun!

Pretty soon breakfast and chores were over,

and Poetry and I were in our warm clothes and boots on our way down the lane to the highway. There wasn't even a car track, because it had snowed for a long time after the party was over the night before. It was certainly a pretty day and not even very cold, with the sun shining and everything.

"Look," I said to Poetry. "Here is where I had the scuffle last night with whoever it was, and here is where he knocked the living daylights out of me."

We both looked and could see where there was a big dent in the snowdrift, but it was nearly filled with snow again. Poetry walked over to where I'd landed on my head and started digging around in the snowdrift with his boots, shuffling the snow this way and that.

I said, "What are you doing that for?"

Poetry grunted, "I'm looking for a clue."

"A clue?" I said. "What for? What kind of a clue?"

"Oh, anything to prove that old John Till did write that note."

I'd already about decided it couldn't have been John Till, so I said to Poetry, "Didn't we see *shoe* tracks last night here in the snow? And when we caught John Till, he had *boots* on, didn't he? And besides, I think Shorty Long's dad wrote it."

And then Poetry let out a war whoop and made a dive for something his boot had scooped up. There it was in his hand—an envelope that looked exactly like the one I'd taken out of our mailbox just before dark the night before.

Sure enough, it *was* the envelope. Since Poetry had never seen the letter before, I let him read it clear through. And did it make him mad!

"It won't take us long to find out if it was John Till who wrote it," he said. "Here comes Little Tom."

And shuffling along toward us was that little redheaded boy himself. His face was kind of sad, and we both felt sorry for him because he was the only one of our gang who had a dad like that. As you know, Circus's dad used to be an alcoholic but wasn't anymore because he had given his heart to the Lord. The Lord had fixed it for him and made him into a neat guy.

"Hi, Tom Till!" we both said at the same time.

"Hi," he said.

He was carrying his lunch in a tin pail, and all of a sudden I noticed something that made me feel sadder. He was wearing shoes that were a lot too big for him, which meant that his parents either couldn't afford to buy him new ones when he needed them or for some other reason he had to wear an old pair of his dad's or brother's. That can happen when a boy's dad won't live the right kind of a life or won't work the way he ought to.

Little Tom acted kind of bashful. But because he was a great little guy, we forgave him for having an alcoholic for a dad, which he couldn't help anyway. So we chatted along, not mentioning the night before at all.

I kept looking at his big flopping shoes, and I thought he was pretty brave to wear them if he had to and not say anything about it or act as if he was ashamed. All of a sudden I wished I was grown up and had a lot of money and could buy shoes for all the boys and girls in the world who needed them and couldn't afford them. Also I wished, so hard it made me mad, that I could make everybody quit making and selling and drinking whiskey and beer and stuff—beer being almost as bad as whiskey, Dad says, because it helps create an appetite for whiskey.

Suddenly Poetry stopped walking and said, "I forgot my report card. What'll Mr. Black say? He was mad at me yesterday for not bringing it."

I'd taken mine the day before, so I didn't have to worry about that, for which I was glad.

"I've got mine," redheaded Tom Till said and pulled it out of his inside coat pocket.

When Tom said that, Poetry spoke up quickly and excitedly. "Who signs yours—your mother or your dad?"

"My dad," Little Tom said. "He's the best writer. Mom can't write very well because of having arthritis in her right hand."

"Let me see your grades," Poetry said.

Little Tom was pretty smart and not ashamed to let anybody see his grades, so he handed the envelope with his report card in it to Poetry.

Almost the second Poetry had it in his

hand, he pulled the card out and looked at the handwriting on it, which I could see said, as plain as day, "John B. Till."

I really felt glad inside, because that handwriting wasn't any more like the awkward writing on the note I'd received the night before than a dog's tracks in the snow are like a chicken's.

I actually sighed out loud when I saw that, because I was glad it wasn't John Till, even though the gang had once beat up on his oldest boy and I had licked the stuffings out of Tom once before he joined our gang.

Poetry looked at me to see if I was looking at the handwriting, which I was, and since he had already read the note a little while before, he grinned to himself and said, "Well, Bill Collins, you're right."

"About what?" Little Tom said.

Poetry had enough sense to say, "You're pretty smart to get such good grades."

"Sure," Little Tom said. "My dad used to be one of the smartest men in the whole country. He still reads an awful lot." Little Tom didn't seem to know anything about what had happened last night, so we didn't tell him.

"Is your dad home?" I said to him.

And he said, "Yep. Came home last night."

Tom seemed sad, though, and I knew it was because his dad had been in jail. Probably any boy who has a dad who has been in jail feels kind of strange inside and ashamed.

We three walked along together in the

snow. I kept wishing Tom had a pair of new shoes or else a pair of nice warm boots to wear, so every now and then I looked down at his too-big shoes, feeling sorry for him.

All of a sudden Poetry gasped out loud, and Tom and I both said at the same time, "'S'matter?" which is what most of us always say to anybody who gasps as he had just done.

Poetry yawned, using one of his mittened hands to half cover up his mouth at the same time, the way you're supposed to do in public when you're trying to be polite. "Nothing," he said. "I just thought of something."

But I knew it must be something important, so he and I just sort of dropped back behind Little Tom. As soon as he had a chance, he said, "Do you see what I've been seeing, Bill Collins?"

"What?" I said.

He said, "Look at those shoe tracks!"

I looked at the tracks Tom Till's shoes were making. And there it was as plain as day—one of the shoes had a hole partway through its sole, and it was leaving a track in the snow exactly like the one we all had seen the night before and had followed to the bridge where it had disappeared.

"So it was Little Tom Till who knocked the living daylights out of you last night at the entrance to our lane!" Poetry said.

"It was not!" I said. "He not only couldn't, but he wouldn't."

Little Tom, who wasn't very far ahead of us,

whirled around and said, "Did one of you guys call me?"

"We were just talking," Poetry yelled up to him, and we all went on, Poetry and I following the tracks.

It certainly was a mystery, I thought.

Then Poetry said to me, "That proves it was old Hook-nose, because those are probably his shoes, and Tom is wearing them to school this morning."

"But old Hook-nose was wearing boots last night, wasn't he?" I said.

Poetry and I sighed to each other and had to stop talking for a while. We had come to Circus's house, and he and a whole flock of girls, who were his sisters, came out to go to school with us.

After that we came to Shorty Long's house, and I felt a tight feeling on the inside of me when he came out. I was remembering the fights I'd had with him, but also tumbling around and over and over in my mind was the Bible verse that Poetry had read at their breakfast table, "Be kind to one another, tenderhearted, forgiving each other, just as God in Christ also has forgiven you."

So, hardly knowing I was going to, I said, "Hi, Shorty!"

He stood stock-still and looked at me, astonished. But I noticed that there was mischief in his eye, as though he was not shocked to hear me using a friendly voice but was pretending to be shocked.

"Hopi, Bopill," he said, which was the crazy new language the Sugar Creek Gang had been using and was called "Openglopish." What he said meant, "Hi, Bill!"

The way to talk Openglopish, you know, is to just put an "op" in front of every vowel sound in every word you say. I didn't like that language very well, especially because of all the trouble I'd had with Shorty Long, who liked it a lot. But I certainly didn't want any more fights, and if it was right for me to make up with him, if I could, and try to get along without fighting, I was going to try to.

So I said to him half cheerfully, "Hopi, Shoportopy Lopong," which is, "Hi, Shorty Long!"

I grinned at him, sort of feeling, though, that it must have been a silly grin.

But there wasn't going to be any chance to make up very soon, I found out, because Shorty Long said to me, "You look like a possum when you grin like that."

I didn't like that at all, remembering what a really sick grin possums get on their faces sometimes. Of course, if Little Jim or Poetry or Big Jim or Circus or Dragonfly had said that to me, I'd have laughed and would have known they didn't mean anything by it. But I have to admit I didn't like it.

So when he said "possum," I remembered the possum that John Till had been skinning the night before at the mouth of the cave, and how I'd thought all along, while we were trail-

ing the man who had knocked the living daylights out of me, that it was the same man who
had written the crazy note in the crazy handwriting, and that of course it was Shorty Long's
dad.

All of a sudden, I felt myself getting hot in
my mind, and I decided to face Shorty Long
with the idea right that minute. So I said to
him, "Your father's handwriting is like a possum's handwriting. It's the craziest, awkwardest
handwriting anybody ever wrote in his life, and
he can't spell for sour apples." I had my right
hand in my outside coat pocket, clasping the
envelope with the letter in it as tight as anything.

"You're crazy," Shorty Long said. "My father
used to teach handwriting. He used to be a
schoolteacher!"

"Oh, he did, did he?" I said. "All right, take
a look at this letter which he shoved in our
mailbox last night." Of course, I didn't know
that it was his dad who had done it, but I
thought I could find out pretty soon if I pre-
tended that his dad had.

I stopped where I was, pulled that envelope
out of my pocket, opened it, and held it out
toward Shorty Long. "Come here, the rest of
you guys," I said.

And Circus and Poetry and Little Jim and
Little Tom Till and I and also Shorty Long
stood reading that crazy note, which somebody
had put in our box.

It took my eyes only a jiffy to go galloping

all the way down the page, reading every word written in that crazy, awkward handwriting. I read the whole thing once more.

When Shorty Long finished reading it, he gasped and had the strangest look on his face. "My dad didn't write that!" he said.

"Oh, he didn't, didn't he?" I said, making up my mind I was going to accuse him of it until he *proved* that his dad didn't. "How do I know he didn't? Didn't Little Jim's parents take your mother to church last Sunday night? And haven't we been beating up on you without half trying? And—"

Shorty Long surprised me then by a very bright but sarcastic remark. "Yes, and aren't you the worst roughneck of the whole Sugar Creek Gang?"

Then Shorty Long made a quick move out of the way of where he thought maybe one of my doubled-up fists was going to land.

But I was just bluffing. For some reason, maybe because Poetry's Bible verse was still sort of holding me back the way a leash holds back a dog from having a fight with another dog, I said, "OK, then, I'm a roughneck. But you'll have to prove that your dad didn't write it."

Shorty Long was pretty smart. He sounded like he had been reading a book written by a lawyer, because he said, "Oh, no, I don't. The burden of proof rests on you. You have to prove that he did. Where's your proof?"

For a minute I was flabbergasted. *I really couldn't prove it, could I?* I thought.

Little Tom Till spoke up then. "Maybe he's got his dad's handwriting on his report card."

Well, that was a good idea. Shorty Long shoved one of his big hands into his pocket and pulled out his report card. It was signed by Delbert Long, who was his dad, and the handwriting was a slanting, jerky writing that wasn't any more like the writing on the letter than the man in the moon looks like a giraffe. And it looked to have been written by an intelligent person who certainly would be able to spell better than whoever *had* written it.

Well, that was that. We all saw both handwritings at the same time and knew that it wasn't Shorty Long's dad's or Little Tom Till's dad's. *Then who did it?* I wondered.

Without planning to be polite, I said to Shorty Long—and I guess I know why I said it—I said, "I'm sorry, Shorty. But who *did* do it?"

And he said, "Whoever did is going to get into trouble if I ever find out who he is!"

Shorty Long whirled away from us, scooped up a big handful of snow, made it into a ball, got a fierce look on his face, and said, "If I knew who did it, I'd knock the living daylights out of him! The dirty crook!"

He swung his arm wide and threw the snowball terribly hard toward the schoolhouse, which wasn't very far from where we all were right that minute. It sailed high, over the heads of the girls who were up ahead of us, and I could see it was going straight for the blue-gray schoolhouse door.

I don't know what made me do it, but for some reason I reached out my hand as if I were trying to stop that snowball, only of course it was too late. I couldn't help but remember the snowball *I'd* thrown the day before, which had gone whizzing straight for that same door. The door had opened, and our teacher, Mr. Black, had stooped down to adjust the doormat. My ball had struck him right on his half-bald head.

My hand was still out, as if I had thrown the ball myself. I didn't have time to wonder what would happen if the door would open again like that, for just that second it did. There our new man teacher stood, bareheaded, his big round face looking sort of blank. He had a rope in his hand, which was the bell rope, and he was getting ready to pull it to let us all know how much time we had before we had to come in and take our seats and get to work.

Then Shorty Long's snowball struck *ker-wham-smash* against Mr. Black's chin. *Ker-smack* against his chin!

And almost before he had had a chance to get over being stunned by the snowball, Mr. Black called out, "All right, William Collins! You can come in and take your seat. That's a fine way to start your second day of school— just like you started your first one. Hurry up!"

That just burned me up! I hadn't thrown the snowball, and I could prove it by all the gang. Shorty Long had done it. I was just getting ready to holler to Mr. Black and say so, when the words kind of caught in my throat. I seemed to be like a dog on a leash again, and Poetry's Bible verse was holding me back. For some reason I wasn't mad at Shorty anymore, because it looked as if whoever had written the letter had just been trying to stir up trouble for all of us.

Another thing that my dad had always taught me was not to be a tattletale, and nobody in a school likes a tattler, either. So I just shut my teeth and lips tight and pulled my cap down over my eyes and started toward the schoolhouse door as if I was the one who had thrown the snowball.

Another thing that probably made me do it was that Little Jim was there. I knew that if it had been Little Jim, *he* wouldn't have told on Shorty Long. So I decided I wouldn't. Besides, Little Jim's parents were really trying to get Shorty's parents to go to church and to become Christians, which is the same as being saved. I knew it wouldn't help any if I blabbed about Shorty's throwing that snowball. It would be better for Shorty to confess it himself.

There wasn't a one of the girls who had seen Shorty do it—only some of the gang who were there. So I started toward the schoolyard gate, shuffled awkwardly past the old iron pump where we all got our drinking water, and was almost to the porch when Dragonfly, who liked me a lot, yelled to Mr. Black, "Mr. Black, Bill didn't throw—"

That was as far as he got. I whirled around quick and yelled "Keep still!"

And Dragonfly kept still.

I went on into the schoolhouse ahead of everybody else, all by myself.

9

It didn't feel very good to have to go into our one-room schoolhouse all alone, not knowing what might happen to me. I felt sick in the pit of my stomach. But I hadn't any more than taken my seat when I heard Mr. Black say at the door behind me, "All right, all you boys of the Sugar Creek Gang, come on in, all of you. The rest of you may play or do anything you like. Hurry up."

There certainly wasn't any mad scramble as there sometimes is when the gang makes a dive for the one and only door of the schoolhouse. Instead, it took almost a whole minute for all the gang to get in. For a while it seemed there was a fight with words out there, for I heard one of the gang say, "You are not! You never joined! You can't go in! He wants just the Sugar Creek Gang!" "Aw, let him come in if he wants to." That was Dragonfly's voice, I knew, and I guessed he and maybe Poetry were in a word fight. One of them was trying to keep Shorty Long from coming in because he didn't belong to the gang, and the other one was trying to let him in. Dragonfly was the only one of the gang who kind of liked Shorty Long. Then I heard Shorty say, "I'm coming in! I don't want to stay out here with all these crazy girls."

Well, I didn't like most girls very well, but I still didn't want anybody to call them crazy. I had a baby sister, and my mother used to be a girl herself. Besides, Circus had one sister who wasn't even a little bit crazy, and she was the main reason that Shorty Long and I had had a fight the day before.

Mr. Black decided it for us when he said, "*All* of the boys come on in and hurry up."

In they all came, going to their different-sized seats in different parts of the room, and Mr. Black went to the front.

I could see behind him, just above his head, the switches he had cut yesterday and had put on a little ledge above the maps of the world. He had a very set face. He stood there looking out over the room at all of us until we were very quiet. I could feel that something was coming—something very interesting but something I was afraid I wouldn't like very well.

Then he spoke, and I certainly was surprised at how calm his voice was, even though it didn't sound very friendly. "We will forget about the snowball William Collins threw at me a minute ago. What I want to do now is something else. I need to know something. In the first place, I'm having it understood right now that *I* am running this school. I am not going to have a gang of boys throwing snowballs at me, insulting me, and writing threatening letters!"

What? I thought. *What does he mean by that? What does he know about a threatening letter?*

He stopped and looked at all of us, letting his sharp bluish-gray eyes flash from one to the other of us. Our faces must have looked blank to him from what he said after that. Mine couldn't have been very blank though, for I was wondering how he knew someone had written a threatening letter and shoved it into our mailbox.

"Well?" he said, with a question mark on the end of his voice and on his face. "Don't look so innocent. Which one of you boys wrote this?"

I looked up at him, and in his hand he was holding an envelope that was the same size and looked exactly like the one that somebody had put in our mailbox, and which somebody had knocked out of my hand at Poetry's lane, and which Poetry had found that morning, and which we had showed to Shorty Long.

I quickly shoved my hand into my pocket to see if I still had my letter, and I did. Yet there it was in Mr. Black's hand right in front of our eyes! He was still looking at us and especially at me, when he said, "Which one of you boys wrote this?" And when nobody answered, he said, "Speak up! Who wrote this?"

Not a one of us spoke up, and I certainly didn't know what to think.

Big Jim raised his hand then, as a boy does in school when he wants to say something or ask something.

Mr. Black looked at him as though he couldn't believe his eyes, and then said, "I'm certainly surprised at you, James! You, of all persons! Will you step up here to the platform, please?"

Big Jim dropped his hand and said, "I never saw it before. I raised my hand because I wanted to ask you to let us see it."

Mr. Black grunted and looked at us all again the way maybe a bear would look at a boy or a gang of boys it would be glad to eat up.

"I suppose you boys know that you can all be arrested for writing letters like this?"

Big Jim looked across to me and I to him, and I knew he was wondering, *What on earth?* Of course Big Jim didn't know that on the way to school Poetry and I had found the letter that somebody had shoved into my dad's mailbox.

Anyway, there was a tangled-up expression on all our faces until suddenly Mr. Black said fiercely, as if he was trying to catch us in a trap, "You boys can either confess, or every one of you will take a switching within the next eight minutes—one minute for each of you!"

His jaw was set grimly. Then he reached up to the top of the maps, took down two switches, laid one of them on the desk, and stepped out to the edge of the platform. The other switch was in one hand and the letter in the other.

Then he looked at us all again. This time he changed his voice and said almost kindly, "I'll give you all one more chance, boys. Anybody want to confess?"

Not a one of us said anything, so he looked across at me and said, "How about you, William Collins? Ever see this before?"

I had my hand in my pocket on the letter I had there, so I said, "No sir, I never did. Anyway I don't think so. I mean—"

And I knew that if I'd been Mr. Black and a boy had said that to me, I'd have thought he was lying.

"Fine," Mr. Black said. "Anybody else want to confess? How about you, Leslie? Have you ever seen this?"

Poetry looked at me, and since he didn't know but what it *might* have been the same letter he had found that morning and that maybe I had given it to Mr. Black, he said, "I-I don't know. I don't think so . . . maybe I have."

"Anybody else? How about you?" He looked at Circus, and Circus looked right straight in front of him and said, "I never saw it before."

"And you, William?" He looked at Shorty Long, and Shorty Long looked at me out of the corner of his eye and said, "Yes sir, Mr. Black. I have."

"Would you mind telling us *where* you saw it, William?"

Shorty Long looked at me again and then at Mr. Black and said, "I saw it in Bill Collins's hand."

Like a flash, Mr. Black turned to me and said, "Will you stand up, young man, and tell us all you know about this—this dastardly bit of cowardice—this cheap way of doing things?"

I sat still in my seat.

"Stand up!" he ordered again, and I could see his face was white with anger.

I stood up.

"Tell us all you know about this letter."

"I don't know anything about it," I said. "I never saw it before."

"You did too," Shorty Long said. "You showed it to me yourself."

"I did not," I said.

I wasn't getting along very well with the plan I'd had in my mind to forgive Shorty Long and be kind to him and everything. Right that minute I was mad at him again and wanted to sock him on the jaw or somewhere. And I could tell by the way I felt that it would take me quite a long time to get over being angry. I'd have to watch my temper pretty close, or I'd say something fierce to him.

I had my hand in my pocket, holding on tight to the letter there, trying to decide what to do with it. Maybe I ought to pull it out and walk right up to Mr. Black and say, "I don't know what's in the letter you have in your hand, but here is one somebody wrote to me." But I felt kind of the way I do in a dream sometimes when a bear is after me and I want to run and can't. I just stood there and looked at Mr. Black and at the letter in his hand.

I guess maybe he had made up his mind to ask each one of us the same question, for right that second he looked at Dragonfly and said, "And you, Roy, do you know anything about this letter?"

And Dragonfly's eyes started to blink as though he was going to be allergic to even the question Mr. Black had asked, but he quickly grabbed his nose, and only a very small part of his sneeze came out. It must have hurt his sty though, because right on the tail end of his sneeze he said, "Ouch!" just as he had when we were sitting on the stairway at Poetry's house and Mr. Black had seen him and frowned at him.

Dragonfly started blinking again, and I knew another sneeze was getting ready to happen. But he stopped all of it this time and said, "No sir," to Mr. Black.

Little Jim was next.

"All right, James," Mr. Black said to Little Jim. "Of course, you don't know anything about this letter?"

And that little guy not only surprised all of us, but he startled us plenty when he said, "My mother has envelopes that color and just that size. I can tell you if it's her handwriting if you'll let me see it."

Of course it didn't even make sense that Little Jim's mom had written such a letter as Mr. Black acted like was written in that envelope.

There was only one of us left, and that was Little Tom Till. All of us looked to where he sat next to the window right behind the big dictionary, which lies on a shelf fastened to the wall.

"All right, Thomas, you're the only one left who didn't do it," Mr. Black said. The very way he said it sounded as though he thought the whole gang of us were telling lies but were acting innocent.

Little Tom sat there looking down at his hands and twisting the handkerchief that was in one of them. Tom didn't answer, so Mr. Black asked him straight out, "Thomas, did you write this?"

Little Tom Till sniffled as though he was going to cry or was already crying. Then he swallowed and all of a sudden spoke up, saying, "No sir, I didn't!"

Right that second Big Jim's hand was waving in the air again, so Mr. Black nodded to him and said, "All right, James!"

Big Jim slid out of his seat, stood up, and in a very gentlemanlike voice, which he nearly always used anyway when he was talking to an older person, said politely, "Mr. Black, I wonder if you will let us see the letter or else read it to us. Most of us don't know anything about it, and we would like to know what it's all about."

Well, when Big Jim used such a kind voice, I remembered one of the Bible verses my dad had made me learn once, "A gentle answer turns away wrath." It means that if anybody is mad at you, you can sometimes keep him from hurting you and can even make his anger melt away like a piece of ice on a hot stove if you will just use a kind voice to him.

Mr. Black looked out over the schoolroom at all of us, and then, maybe without intending to, he used the same kind of kind voice that Big Jim had used. He said: "How many of you boys have never seen this letter? Raise your hands, please."

Well, I raised my freckled hand, Dragonfly raised his awkward, little-bit-dirty one, Circus raised his very brown one, Big Jim raised his big one, Little Jim raised his small hand, which he always kept very clean because his mom made him wash his hands a lot since he practiced the piano every day. Only Shorty Long and Little Tom and Poetry didn't have their hands up.

Well, I knew that Poetry hadn't seen it but only thought he had. Of course, I didn't know whether Shorty Long had seen it or not, because I still wondered if maybe his dad had been the one who had written the one I had in my pocket. If he wrote the one I had in my pocket, maybe he also wrote the one that was in Mr. Black's hand.

I was surprised at Little Tom, though, but maybe he didn't understand the question.

"All right," Mr. Black said all of a sudden. He whirled around and walked up to the platform where he could look out over the schoolroom at all of us and see all of us at the same time without having to move his head in different directions. "I'll read it to you."

I quickly grabbed a piece of paper and a pencil and was going to try to write it down while he read it.

When he spied me doing that, it must have given him a bright idea, for he said to all of us, "I'll not only read it to you, boys, but I'm going to ask each one of you to take it down just as I give it to you. I'll soon find out which one of you wrote it!"

And that's how the mystery began to get even worse than it had been. Things began to make a little sense as I wrote, though, following along behind Mr. Black's very gruff voice. The letter must have made him angry while he was reading it to us, because the farther he read, the more gruff his voice became. In fact it sounded terribly angry. The letter started out: "Dear Hoosier Schoolmaster."

He didn't read very fast because of waiting for the slowest ones of us to follow him, so I had a moment's time for my mind to go hop-skip-and-jump over toward Poetry. I was remembering the book he had in his library, which we had been reading last night about the Hoosier schoolmaster who had a gang of rough boys in his school. Of course, I knew that Poetry had not written any such crazy letter.

Mr. Black's voice went on, and I began to write what he read:

> You are not going to get anywhere by stirring up trouble in the Sugar Creek Gang. You are a roughneck and to blame for all the trouble we had yesterday . . .

While I was writing that, I happened to think that whoever had written the note must have written it some time after school yesterday, because no one could have written anything about the day before it was over. The next thing Mr. Black read for us to write was:

> If you expect to get along with the boys of the Sugar Creek Gang, you will have to apologize for what you did yesterday . . .

Whew! I thought. *Whoever wrote that certainly had a lot of nerve.*

We kept on writing, and this is what came next—and was even worse than what I'd already written:

> We are not used to having a baldheaded schoolteacher boss us around. If you want to apologize like a gentleman, meet us at the Sugar Creek bridge on the North Road between six and seven o'clock tonight. If you don't, there will be more trouble tomorrow.
>
> THE GANG
>
> P. S. If you get there before we do, wait till we come.

Just as soon as we had finished what he'd read to us, Mr. Black made us all come to the platform and lay our papers down side by side on the wide top of his big rectangular desk. Then he made us stand all around his desk beside and behind him and look at the different handwriting to see which one was like the one he had in his hand.

There wasn't one that was like it. But it *was*

exactly like the handwriting on the letter in my pocket. It was the same kind of stationery too, just an ordinary kind you buy in any store, having blue lines on it for your pencil or pen to follow.

I still had my letter in my pocket and was wondering if I ought to show it to Mr. Black, when Big Jim spoke very politely again, although his voice was trembling; "Where did you find this, Mr. Black?"

I was proud of Big Jim, and I remembered that under the bridge last night he had said it would be up to us to prove to Mr. Black we were not roughnecks.

Mr. Black answered as respectfully as Big Jim had asked the question. "It was tucked under the pommel coat-strap on my saddle, when I went out to take a ride."

Then Big Jim said, "Of course, you know now that none of the Sugar Creek Gang wrote it."

All of a sudden I pulled the other note out of my pocket and tossed it down on the desk and said, "And here is another note somebody wrote."

We all stood there while Mr. Black opened the envelope and read the insulting words, which were written in the same handwriting as that in the letter he had found on his saddle. While he was reading, a strange expression came over his face. I noticed his eyes take on a faraway look, while he lifted his head and stared toward the window as if he wasn't seeing anything. He didn't even look at us when he said, "You may take your seats, boys," which we did.

He walked around in front of his desk, looked down at us, and said, "It's past time for school to begin. Ring the bell, Leslie," which Poetry started to do right away.

"Wait," Mr. Black said to him, and Poetry waited. He had already reached the door, had the bell rope in his hand, and was just ready to give it a long hard pull.

"Boys," Mr. Black said, "I think you and I had a bad start yesterday. I don't know who is responsible, but I am going to ask that we begin all over again, not only as teacher and pupils but as friends. Evidently someone is trying to stir up trouble for us all. Let's keep our eyes open during the next few days to see if we can find out who is doing it."

Poetry still had the bell rope in his hand, and everything was very quiet in the room for a minute while Mr. Black just stood there and looked at us. In one hand he had the two letters and in the other the switches he had taken down a little while before. Then he moved back to the maps, put both switches on the ledge above them, turned back to us, and said, "I have a notion we are not going to need those switches. All right, Leslie—"

And right away I heard the squeaking of the wheel in the belfry and the clanging of the big school bell. Then I felt the shaking of the windows of the schoolhouse as the bell was ringing. Right away there were a lot of steps on the porch, the door opened, a flock of noisy girls came in, and school started.

Somehow I had a very light feeling inside, as if the Bible verses Poetry and I had read that morning had made me feel all white where it had been kind of black before. And I knew that maybe I was going to like our new teacher a whole lot.

10

Well, it was kind of a long day, but we didn't have any more trouble, not even with Shorty Long. At four o'clock we were all out, and the gang was hurrying as fast as we could go toward Poetry's house. Most of our parents had said we could meet there first before going up to Old Man Paddler's cabin with all the good things to eat that had been left over from the party.

At Poetry's house, his mom told me I could go too because she had called up my dad, who was home again, and told him about what the parents had decided the night before. And Dad had said, "All right," but I was to get home as quick after supper as I could. It would get dark early, and none of our parents wanted us to be out after dark.

"It's bound to get dark before we can get home, though," Big Jim said, so we took Poetry's lantern with us. I also took Dad's flashlight, which I had left at Poetry's house. Besides, we would need lights to go through the cave.

Pretty soon all of us—except Tom Till, whose dad had told him to come home right after school—were on our way down through the woods from Poetry's, going toward the sycamore tree and the cave.

We had plenty of time, so we went past the Sugar Creek bridge and stopped awhile to look around. But all our tracks of the night before were covered up.

We looked in the woodchuck den where the skunk had been caught and killed, and Circus said to Poetry, "I stopped and got it on the way home from your house last night."

Poetry said, "I *thought* you smelled like a skunk all day today." But it wasn't very funny.

We walked along the crest of the hill for a while till we came to the place where the boot tracks had gone out toward Bumblebee Hill. But all of them, including ours, were covered with snow.

"I think I know who wrote those crazy letters," Poetry said. He was the one of the gang who planned to be a real detective someday and was already smarter than any of us when it came to having ideas about who had done what and why.

"Who did?" some of us asked him.

He said, "Just wait and see. I'll bet we find out tonight."

"Whyn't you tell us now?" Dragonfly wanted to know.

Poetry said, "Wait'll we get to Old Man Paddler's cabin, and I will."

At the old sycamore tree with the long opening in its side, we stopped and looked around. It was big enough for two of us boys to crawl into one at a time and stand in side by side. Little Jim had his stick, which smelled nice and clean because he had washed it with soap at his house, and he was swishing it around at everything. Circus looked at the different trees as if he wanted to climb one of them but also didn't want to because of its not being any fun to climb a cold tree with snow on its trunk. Big Jim had a grim look on his face as though he was a bit worried. He looked around at the place where we had all had our wrestling match with old John Till, but there weren't any tracks left there either because it had snowed so much after the fight.

Dragonfly was grinning, but he also seemed to be trembling a little. I thought maybe he was cold and wished we'd hurry up and go through the dark cave and get to Old Man Paddler's nice warm cabin. Although it wasn't that cold, especially when a boy has been walking or running and has on warm clothes, which Dragonfly did.

Poetry borrowed Little Jim's stick and began to swish it around in the snow where we'd had our fight with John Till.

I said, "What are you doing that for?"

He said, "Looking for another clue—maybe another crazy letter. Maybe John Till dropped another one here in the fight."

"But John Till didn't write them," I said. "I wish you would stop thinking he did. I wish—"

Poetry interrupted me. "I wish you would stop wishing that I would stop thinking." Then he started a poem, which was the first one he had quoted to us all day, which meant he was feeling very fine and mischievous again. He said:

> "There was a young turkey
> Who was feeling quite perky
> Because he was getting so fat,
> But when he found out
> Thanksgiving was near,
> He wished he was thin as a rat."

Poetry didn't find anything, so we went on up to the big canvas curtain that hangs in front of the entrance to the cave. I had a weird feeling in my mind and around my heart that we were going to run into another exciting adventure almost right away, and maybe we would meet it in that dark cave on the way through to Old Man Paddler's cabin.

Big Jim must have felt the same way, for he stopped us by lifting his finger to his pursed lips and saying, "*Sh!* Quiet, everybody."

Everybody was quiet.

Then he said, "Whoever has been writing notes and putting them around the neighborhood to stir up trouble for us is bound to be somebody who knows us and doesn't like us. Whoever he is, he knows this neighborhood pretty well, for he knew how to get to the cave in the dark and put Bill's suitcase there."

Big Jim and Circus led the way, using Poetry's lantern and my dad's big long flashlight. The rest of us followed along behind, one at a time in Indian fashion. The passage was too narrow in some places for two of us to walk side by side without bumping into each other too much. Sand and gravel covered the solid rock floor, and the cave had a rock roof.

Our parents had inspected the cave a long time ago and decided it was safe for us to go through. They didn't want us ever to go into or play in a cave that had only a dirt roof, because it might cave in on us and kill us or smother us as that kind of cave sometimes does, which you read about in newspapers. But ours had a rock roof, and so it was safe.

I was disappointed that we didn't run into any new mystery on the way through the cave, but we didn't. And in just a few minutes we came to the big wooden door at the other end. We knocked, and in a moment a quavering old voice called, "Who's there?"

When we said, "The Sugar Creek Gang," right away we heard another door opening and knew it was Old Man Paddler lifting up the trapdoor to his cellar. Then we heard him come down his wooden steps to the big door where we were and heard a key turning in the big lock. Right away we were in the cellar and up the stairs and in his cabin, putting down the trapdoor.

Boy, oh, boy, it felt good to be in that kind old man's cabin again with the nice warm fire crackling in the fireplace and the teakettle sitting on the stove. Everything looked just as neat and clean as if he had a wife to keep it clean but no boys to make it dirty.

"Well, well, well, boys," he said, when we first came in. "What do you have there in that basket?"

"Surprise," some of us said at the same time.

He sat in a homemade chair at his table by the window, and the sun, which was getting ready to set behind a hill, was shining in on his very white hair and long white beard.

"Oh," he said, "a picnic supper! That's fine! Well, just make yourselves at home. You may put the water on for sassafras tea. I think I'll finish this letter I'm writing first."

Little Jim nudged me, and I knew he felt good, because he liked sassafras tea better than anything else to drink when we were at Old Man Paddler's cabin.

"There isn't any water," Circus said, looking into an empty pail on a washstand over by the back door, which was also the front door.

The old man lifted his fine head, scratched it just behind the right ear with a long yellow pencil, and said, "So there isn't. I've been using snow water—haven't had a chance to scoop a path down to the spring yet."

That was what my dad would have called an "indirect method" of saying to a gang of boys, "Some of you scoop a path from the door to the spring, some of you carry a pail or two of water, and anybody who wants to can do anything else he wants to, if it needs to be done!"

In fact Dad had been using that method on me at our house for a while. Instead of saying,

"Bill, you're acting awfully lazy today. Get out and gather the eggs," he might say, "By the way, Bill, I noticed that old Bent Comb was on the nest under the barn again today. Doesn't she know that's the coldest place on earth to leave an egg and that it'll freeze and crack and be no good for selling to help buy a boy's new sled? You'd think old Bent Comb would know her egg would freeze if it happened to stay in the nest too long!"

And I'd say to Dad, "I'll go gather the eggs," which I would nearly always do right away.

Anyway, when Old Man Paddler said what he said, Poetry and I made a dive for a snow shovel in the corner by the door. Then we went to get the big scoop shovel that we knew he kept in a small woodshed not far from the cabin. And in a jiffy we were scooping away.

Circus didn't wait for us to get a path shoveled but went leaping and galloping out through the drifts to the spring, which was at the foot of a small hill and at the end of a path we knew was there in the summertime—and which we were trying to follow while we were shoveling right that minute.

Different ones of the rest of the gang did different things, such as stir up the fire in the fireplace and in the cookstove, carry in more wood and stack it in a little rack against the wall beside the fireplace, and make and throw snowballs at different things around the old man's place.

Poetry and I were grunting along, shoveling as fast as we could and feeling fine because it's the best feeling in the world to get warm inside your warm clothes when you are working on a cold day. You don't feel cold because you're working, and you feel especially fine when you can see the path getting longer and longer while you work.

Pretty soon, though, I said to Poetry, "'S'matter? What's the worry on your face for?"

And he said, "Did you see what I saw?"

"No—what?" I said.

"Did you notice what kind of stationery he was writing his letter on? That—that old-fashioned writing tablet?"

I guess I hadn't noticed, although it's a wonder I hadn't. Because if there was anything in the world I was interested in, it would be anything anybody would write using the same kind of stationery somebody had written on and shoved into our mailbox—and also the same kind of stationery somebody had written on and tucked under the pommel coat-strap of Mr. Black's saddle.

"But," I said to Poetry, "certainly Old Man Paddler wouldn't write such crazy letters. Besides, he wouldn't knock me down. Also, he can't run, and he doesn't wear that kind of shoes."

"Of course not," Poetry said. "I didn't say he did, did I? But I know who did."

Well, he wouldn't tell me what he knew, so pretty soon we had our path scooped to the spring and were back in the nice warm cabin with the fire crackling in the fireplace and the teakettle singing on the stove. The sun was already down. As I looked out toward the west where it had been, there were about seven very pretty rows of reddish clouds hanging nearly all the way across the sky. They looked like seven very long rails in the fence that is just across the road from our house.

The old man had lit a lamp while we were outside, and it was on the table beside him now. He was just about to finish his letter. On the stove was a little granite pan nearly filled with steaming reddish water and red chips of sassafras roots.

"I'll just sign my name," he said, "and then it'll be ready for mailing. Bob will be here any minute now to mail it for me. He's going to town tonight, and this letter has to get off on the midnight train. He's taking the same train back to his job at Boulderville."

And right that second it was just like somebody had turned on a big electric light in my mind. Why, of course, *that* was who had written those letters—Big Bob Till! He must have come home for a day or two to see his dad, who had just got out of jail, and was still mad at the Sugar Creek Gang, as he had always been. He probably had tried to get us all into trouble by writing to Mr. Black, trying to make him hate the Sugar Creek Gang, and by writing that crazy note to my dad, which would make it look like Shorty Long's dad had written it, just to get

Shorty and me mad at each other. Why, it was as plain as the crooked nose on Dragonfly's pop-eyed face that Big Bob Till had done it.

"Bob Till?" different ones asked the old man at the same time.

Poetry looked at me and grinned, and the grin said, *I told you so.*

And Old Man Paddler said, "Yes, Bob has been home for several days while his father is out on parole. Bob's been staying here part of the time. There's a boy who needs a friend, boys—somebody to be a real father to him. If we don't be kind to him, he'll turn out to be a very, very bad boy and a menace to society.

"Now, while we're waiting for the tea to get done, do you want to hear my letter to my brother—my twin brother down in Palm Tree Island, you know?"

Well, we did, and we didn't. Most of us wanted to talk to each other first, especially Poetry, who whispered to me, "I'll bet Bob's dad was waiting at the bridge for him in their old car last night. When Bob got there, old John Till, who had boots on, must have climbed out and started running the trapline. Bob probably had on a shoe with a hole in its sole, and he got in and drove the car home. Then this morning Little Tom borrowed his brother Bob's shoes and wore them to school—I figured it out myself."

I was sure Poetry was right. But because it was the only polite thing to do, we listened to Old Man Paddler's letter to his twin brother:

Dear Brother Kenneth,

I am so pleased that you are planning to come home. I can hardly wait until I see you again. I think, though, because you have been ill and because the weather is very cold here and you are accustomed to a warm climate, you had better wait till spring before you come . . .

Boy, oh, boy, I was excited, with the mystery of the crazy letters solved, and at the same time remembering how exactly alike Old Man Paddler and his twin brother looked, and thinking what fun it was going to be when those two nice old gentlemen got to see each other for the first time in a lot of years. Imagine those two long-whiskered men living in this little old weather-beaten cabin and both of them friends of the Sugar Creek Gang!

The letter was rambling on when I heard somebody knock downstairs on the big wooden door, and I knew it was Bob Till. I looked at Big Jim's face and noticed that he had his lips pressed close together. I also noticed that his fists were doubled up. He looked right straight into my eyes and said, "No fighting, Bill. Let me handle him."

Then Big Jim jumped up and lifted the trapdoor to the cellar and dashed down to open the other door to let in Bob Till, his worst enemy.

I don't know what I expected to happen when Big Jim and Big Bob met in Old Man

Paddler's cellar. They'd been enemies for a long time and had had two fierce fights. One was on Bumblebee Hill, and the other was at the top of the iron stairway in an elevated station in Chicago, where Bob had fallen down and cut a gash in his head. It was Big Jim who had saved his life when they had to take Bob to a hospital for a blood transfusion. Big Jim's and Bob's blood were the same type.

But even though Big Jim had given his blood for him, still Bob didn't like him and was always doing everything he could to cause Big Jim and the whole Sugar Creek Gang trouble.

My heart was pounding, and I noticed my own fists were doubled up as I listened hard to learn what would happen. Big Jim could easily knock the living daylights out of Bob if he got to hit him first, but Bob was a fierce fighter too, so . . .

Then I heard that great oak door down there open and Big Jim's voice say politely, "Come in, Bob. Supper's ready upstairs. The whole gang is here, and we're having a surprise supper on Old Man Paddler."

And then I heard a lot of different kinds of noise down there. I heard sounds like somebody's hand grabbing a doorknob and then feet scuffling on the hard dirt floor of the cellar. And then Bob's voice said, "Oh, no, you don't, Big Jim! You yellow-livered coward. Take that and that and that! You will tell on my dad, will you, and get him sent back to jail?"

And then there was more noise and a

sound like twenty feet on the floor at the same time, then a terrible bang as the cellar door slammed shut. And then I heard somebody's feet go *crunch, crunch, crunchety-crunch-crunch-crunch* on the gravel of the floor of the cave, and I guessed it was Bob Till running away.

I certainly was on my feet in a hurry, and so was the rest of the gang. We almost stumbled over each other on our way down that stairway to where we found Big Jim lying facedown on the dirt floor right close to the heavy oak door.

"We'll get him—the coward!" Circus said. He had my dad's flashlight in his hand, and I knew he was the fastest runner of the gang. He knew every inch of the way through the cave and could probably catch Bob before he got through to the cave entrance or at least in a little while after they came out at the other end.

Big Jim groaned, rolled over, and sat up right in the place where the door would have to open if Circus opened it, and he said, "No! Let him go. I don't want to hurt him . . ." Big Jim's voice kind of faded away as if he was feeling very weak. Then all of a sudden he toppled over, the way a tree does when you've chopped it off at the roots, and he fell on his face again.

I simply have to wind up this story right here, without taking time to tell you how we revived Big Jim and how we had our party after he felt better, and how we ourselves mailed Old Man Paddler's letter to his brother on Palm Tree Island.

But when we were on the way home and

Poetry and Little Jim and I were together, Little Jim piped up with something that was just like the things he is always saying and thinking: "Big Jim gave his blood for Bob in Chicago once, and now he is trying to be kind to him. But Bob is still mean. It's just like what happened in the Bible, I'll bet. Somebody gave His blood on the cross for John Till and Bob, and they're running away from Him too."

And I knew Little Jim was right.

As Poetry and I parted at his gate, he said to me, "Remember the story we read last night in *The Hoosier Schoolmaster*?"

I said, "Sure, can't forget it. Why?"

"Oh, nothing, but I was wondering if a board put on the top of a chimney when there was a fire in the stove would make the stove smoke like it says in the book. Do you suppose it would?"

I looked at him, and he looked at me, and I sort of knew that way back in the mischievous part of his mind there was an idea that before long would probably stir up something very interesting in the Sugar Creek School.

The *Sugar Creek Gang* Series: